MW01101909

The Children
Are Revolting

Enjoy !

Jon Turley

Turley Tales

The Children Are Revolting

Jon Turley

First edition published by The Robinswood Press, 2003.

Design and layout by Steve Emms.
Illustrations © Susan Hellard 2003.
Printed by Latimer Trend Ltd., Plymouth.

The Robinswood Press

Stourbridge England

ISBN 1-869981-774

Revolution

Pay-back

Dark Times

Resolution

Dedication

For my beautiful wife, Helen...
   ...*joy!*

About the Author

Jon Turley has an unquenchable thirst for writing. He loves creating stories packed with action, mystery and intrigue.

Jon grew up in Worcester, England, where he attended the Royal Grammar School. After going to University in Cheltenham, he became a Primary School Teacher and taught in Dudley, England and in Dubai.

He currently lives in England with his wife, Helen. He adores animals and likes nothing better than being taken for a walk by his over-energetic dog, 'Jet'. Many a time he's thought up a storyline or invented a character whilst sitting on the top of the Malvern Hills or rambling deep inside the Bewdley Forest.

Other titles by Jon Turley from The Robinswood Press include *The Doomed Prince*, *The R.A.T.T. Pack* and *Empty Pages*.

Revolution

Chapter 1

A Revolting Episode

Rather nervously, Devinia Longchamps, the School Secretary, wobbled past the other members of staff. She entered the corridor outside the Staffroom – but froze immediately. A soft gooey lump came hurtling from one of the catapults and caught her on the side of the head. Laughter followed from the children on the balcony which overlooked the scene. The staff protested. But all they got in return was the usual "Nuts!" from Arty Fox.

Devinia Longchamps managed to hold back her tears as she entered her own Office and raced to the Headmaster's door. She knocked and entered without waiting for a reply. Godfrey Randolph Mannering was sitting behind his large oak desk, his feet up, snoozing. He woke with a start. Looking around the room, he tried to focus on where he was and who had so rudely interrupted him. He saw Miss Longchamps standing there and tutted.

"I say, Miss Longchamps, you could have knocked before entering, you know. I was in the middle of some important school planning!" He chuckled at his rather pathetic joke and picked up his morning newspaper.

"Oh, but Mr Mannering, Sir –" started Devinia.

"What is it, Miss Longchamps? What's the matter?"

"Oh, Sir. It's awful, Sir."

"What's awful? Come on, Miss Longchamps, spit it out!"

"The children, Mr Mannering."

"What about the children?"

"Well... the children are revolting!"

"Absolutely! I couldn't agree more! Little beggars!" replied the Head, still looking at his paper.

"No, Sir, you don't understand! The children *are* revolting!"

"True, true, Miss Longchamps, but don't let it get you down, my dear. A few more weeks and the term will be over. Then you'll be away from that bunch of social deviants! They're nothing more than a pain in the rear, you know!"

"Mr Mannering!" yelled Devinia, sobbing her heart out at this point. "You have to understand, Sir. The children aren't just revolting, they're... *revolting!* They've taken over the school. They have taken us all prisoner!"

"I beg your pardon?" asked the Head, wondering if he'd heard things correctly.

"We're surrounded, Sir! It's a revolt! It's a rebellion! *It's the end!*"

"*What!*" shouted the Head, so loudly that Devinia Longchamps had to cover her ears. "A revolt! In my school. Why didn't you say so, you silly old moo?"

"Well I did try, Sir!" whimpered Devinia. "And I don't wish to be called an 'old moo', thank you very much!"

"Never mind that – *Devinia* – what's all this about a revolt?"

But without waiting for a reply, Godfrey Randolph Mannering stormed out of his Office, through Devinia's Office and into the corridor outside. His black cotton gown flared out from his sides, forced outwards from the air that raced into it by the sheer speed at which he stomped through the rooms. The outspread gown gave the Head the appearance of a vampire swooping down through bedroom windows on his way to another helpless victim. His eyes narrowed and a scowl carved its way into his expression.

The students of West Mayling House, however, were anything but your typical helpless victims. Godfrey Mannering stopped abruptly when he saw young Mitch McGovern standing at one end of the corridor and four settees all piled up at the other. He looked up the stairs at the barricade of desks and chairs and glared at the catapults being held by the students. Godfrey Mannering put his hands on his hips and slowly made his way into the Staffroom. The staff parted like the sea before Moses, leaving the Head looking directly at Arty Fox.

"What's your name, boy?" demanded the Head, pointing at Arty.

"Arthur James Fox... you Muppet!" was the reply.

Jimmy 'Brains' Mahoy, Arty's right-hand man, closed his eyes and cringed at these words. Even though the rebellion was going to plan, he was still very afraid of this Headmaster.

"What did you say, *sonny?*" hissed the Head like a rattlesnake.

"Shut it, Muppet!" retorted Arty. "It's not your turn to talk, it's mine. So keep it zipped, open your eyes and use your loaf... that's if you have anything between those ears of yours."

"Damned cheek!" griped the Head.

Arty leaped out of his chair and over to the wooden cupboard by the wall. He turned round and gave a wry smile to the Head. "Now, just in case you think this is an April Fool prank, let me start by showing you something."

He opened the cupboard doors wide to reveal several battered-looking teachers. First, there was Sebastian Bannister, the PE Teacher. He was looking completely dishevelled from some unusual exertions on the rugby field. Next to appear were Philippe Saint-Moreaux, who taught French, and Barbara Alison, the junior PE Teacher, dressed only in their underclothes. Last was Agnes Brewer, the Cook, still looking slightly green after an unpleasant ordeal with her own home-made cooking!

The Head looked on in disbelief. "What the –"

"Uh, uh, uh!" interrupted Arty. "What did I say about keeping it zipped? It's time to face the facts,

Godfrey. You're surrounded... You're our prisoner... We've taken over the entire school. This rebellion is already one hundred per cent successful. So, I suggest you sit down, pipe down and admit defeat, you... half-brained Teletubby."

"Teletubby, huh? Damned cheek!" snorted the Head as he lumbered towards Arty.

Arty whipped out a catapult from the pocket of his blazer and aimed a mouldy plum at the Head's more delicate regions. "Uh, uh! Where do you think you're going?"

"Damned *cheek!*"

"It's not your *cheeks* I'm aiming at, Godfrey!"

"*Damned* cheek!" he muttered. The Head paused and took a deep breath. "So, you've taken over the school, huh? You've got us all surrounded, huh? You want me to admit defeat, huh? Just remind me – did I really hear you, a miserable little Third Former, say that to me, Headmaster of this school?"

"You did."

"And, may I ask, are you absolutely certain this revolt of yours is going to succeed?"

"Yes."

"Sure about that?"

"Yes, thank you."

"Well, I beg to differ, young... Fox, is it?"

"That's right. Glad you finally remembered. It's Fox, Arthur James Fox. My friends get to call me 'Arty'. You get to call me 'Sir'."

"Is that so? Well, 'Sir', I hate to spoil your little party here, but I have to tell you that I'm not very happy –"

"Pity," interrupted Arty.

"– not very happy *at all*."

"Heart-breaking."

"Yes! The way I feel right now I'd probably pass a *Degree* in Unhappiness.

"Ha, ha."

"Laugh if you want to, Fox, but *I* don't find it funny."

"Shame."

"Yes – isn't it? And talking about shame, let's discuss the shame that *you've* brought upon this school by master-minding all this nonsense!"

"Shame that *we've* brought upon this school?" yelled Arty. "That's a bit rich coming from you, you corrupt old Wrinkly!"

"Corrupt?" bellowed the Head, trying to impose a bit more authority on the whole situation by raising his voice. "How dare you!"

"How dare I? I'll tell you how I dare, you crooked old Crumbly! We know all about your secret meetings, Godfrey. We know all about your plot to embezzle the school's fee money and your plans to make yourselves rich! Oh, yes, *we* know the truth, the whole truth and nothing but the sordid truth!"

Godfrey Mannering was stunned by all these 'truths' coming from Arty's mouth. The other staff stood aghast at the whole situation, trying to fathom out exactly how Arty knew all this. They stood motionless, their mouths wide open with only their eyes darting left to right as they looked anxiously at each other.

The Head kept his hands pressed firmly against his hips, though a nervous twitch made his fingers flinch rapidly and his palms flick open and closed. He looked down at the carpet, then up at the ceiling. He puckered his lips in thought and started to take a few slow paces around. He stopped and glanced quickly at Arty, narrowing his eyes as he did so.

"Just how many of you are involved in this revolt?"

"Every single one of us," came the reply.

"But I have only seen a dozen or so of you here. That means you're a little outnumbered, aren't you?" The Head gave a devious grin.

"I know what you're thinking," smirked Arty. "But – don't go there, girlfriend!"

Ouch! That made the rest of the students giggle nervously. Arty's sarcastic tone was amazing. To them, he didn't seem to be stressed or afraid at all. He seemed to be totally in control, coming out with precisely the right reply at precisely the right time. Deep down, however, Arty was still shaking like a leaf. Now the Head had shown Arty that he might be planning a counter-attack, Arty felt those butterflies fluttering even more in his stomach.

Godfrey Mannering hadn't taken very kindly to that sort of sarcasm. He scowled so menacingly even the other members of staff cowered backwards. One of them even crept behind a settee to hide...

"You cheeky little brat!" bellowed the red-faced Headmaster. "You downright, utter fool! Just whom do you think you're talking to? I'm Godfrey Randolph Mannering, Headmaster of West Mayling House, and I'm going to teach you a lesson you'll never forget. I'm going to cane you and all these other clowns so hard you'll have the name *Mannering* tattooed into your backsides for life!"

He turned to face the Staff. "And as for you, you bunch of wet tissues, don't just stand there! Do something! Get in there and sort them out. Now!"

* * *

Now, admittedly, this is not your average scene inside a Private School on an otherwise warm, sunny Saturday afternoon in Spring. Indeed, you may well be asking yourself: What caused this revolt? Why are there teachers in a cupboard? Why are some of them dressed only in their underwear? How come they all look rather the worse for wear? And what are these so-called 'truths' that Arty Fox had mentioned?

The answers to these questions lie in the past. If we were to turn the clock back, you'd discover how this stand-off between Godfrey Mannering and Arty Fox arose. You'd see why these children acted the way they did.

They didn't start this revolution for nothing. They were adamant that they had a good reason. In fact they were sure they had several. If you knew these reasons, you'd understand why, at four o'clock in the afternoon, Arthur James Fox was calling the awesome Headmaster of his school a 'Muppet'.

So here goes...

Chapter 2

Rebel With A Cause

Arty Fox was a rebel. To phrase it more accurately, Arty Fox *became* a rebel. How it's worded is actually not important. The fact remains that Arty Fox *did* spearhead a rebellion, an uprising, a revolt. It should be recorded here that Arty Fox didn't instigate this revolution without just cause or reason. He simply became one of the main players in an extraordinary sequence of events that were to befall the up till then 'calm waters' of West Mayling House.

These events would have sent shock waves up and down the corridors of every school in the United Kingdom – through every Staffroom, every classroom and every Assembly Hall – had the news of what *really* happened ever become public knowledge.

But the truth never did reach the surface. No-one outside West Mayling ever found out. It all became a hushed whisper, misted over and lost in folklore. Why was the truth never known? What was the truth?

Let me start by explaining what West Mayling House was like – and then I'll tell you how and why the storm clouds started to brew from within...

* * *

West Mayling House was a spectacle to behold. Draped in history, it had a proud reputation that spanned seven hundred and thirty-two years. It had charm, it had elegance and it had grandeur. It stood in one hundred and twenty-five acres of some of the most beautiful countryside in Great Britain. A wall – three metres high – surrounded the entire grounds. The Main Gates of the school were very impressive and boasted the school's shield of arms in the centre. Once you were through these gates, a gravelled pathway crunched beneath your feet as it snaked its way through the school's grounds.

The grounds themselves were also magnificent, stretching all around for as far as the eye could see. Within the grounds stood some fine old oaks, guarding the numerous sporting pitches, the Pavilion, the two heated swimming pools and the new ultra-modern Sports Hall. The lawns were carefully manicured and the bushes evenly cropped. Trees blossomed in the corner of the fields and a spectrum of colourful flowers lined every pathway. The buildings were constructed with Cotswold stone and stood tall, strong and noble. Their windows glistened and sparkled in the sunlight. Just below the roof, stone figures were carved into the masonry, each creepy sculpture watching over the courtyard with its sharp, staring eyes.

The Main Building was a cross between the White

House and Buckingham Palace – with white marble columns supporting a triangular-shaped facade. The arched Front Door was large and forbidding. Attached to the wall alongside was a large, brass plaque with the inscription engraved upon it:

West Mayling House
Boys and Girls 11-14 years
Headmaster Mr G.R. Mannering

Inside the Main Building was the great, square Entrance Hall. A lengthy corridor echoed away into the distance, past the Kitchens and the Dining Hall, eventually leading to the elegant Main Hall. To one side of the Entrance Hall was the School Secretary's Office which led through to the Headmaster's Office. Next door to these was the Staffroom.

Leading up from the opposite side of the Entrance Hall was a beautiful, wide, carved wooden staircase. On the first floor were housed the Old Library and the Staff Quarters. On the second, third and fourth floors were the student Dormitories and Bathrooms.

Walking out of this building, the students would enter a maze of pathways that would take them to their classrooms, and here is where any other school would become very envious. Every room was huge, crammed with all the latest equipment and resources. West Mayling House was, quite simply, a haven for high-tech, cutting-edge, state-of-the-art education!

* * *

It all sounds very impressive, doesn't it? But you shouldn't judge a book by its cover...

It would cost you an arm and a leg to send your beloved offspring to West Mayling House. Money doesn't always buy you the best, though. For, if the school was as beautiful as it seemed, why did Arty Fox feel the need to revolt? It was simple. The truth presented a totally different picture. The day-to-day life of a West Mayling child was not the comfortable, spoilt existence it certainly appeared to be.

To say that the living quarters were a little sparse in décor was more than a slight understatement. Here was where the children spent the best part of their youth, wondering why their parents had sent them away so early on in life.

The First Formers slept in two large rooms on the second floor, one for boys and one for girls. These rooms were like old hospital wards with beds along the walls and an aisle running down the middle. High above each bed was a small round window. To the side of each bed stood a shabby wooden wardrobe with a shaving mirror fixed to the inside. Quite why eleven-year-olds had shaving mirrors was something that the older children could never work out.

The beds were anything but comfortable. The coarse linen sheets grazed elbows and knees, which made turning over at night into a nasty, painful experience. The bed-frames were old and rickety, each one creaking and groaning whenever anyone moved.

The Second Formers were split amongst four adjoining rooms on the third floor. They felt a little superior because they had 'two extra features' – a dressing table and a 'room with a view'. Illusions of splendour were short-lived, however, as the 'view' was mainly over the back of the Kitchens. The scenery was therefore little more than large, round dustbins and the noisy, old generator. Still, perhaps it's the thought that counts!

Only the oldest, the Third Formers, had what the Prospectus described as 'complete privacy on the top floor'. West Mayling had, however, redefined the word 'privacy' by giving it the meaning of 'six to a room'. Each room had six beds, six homework desks, six dressing tables, six wardrobes – still shabby and this time without mirrors. But privilege didn't end there! As well as being able to choose who you shared your room with, Third Formers had two extra treats... a decent view of the school grounds and something to spoil them completely – a ceramic wash basin in the corner by the window. Luxury personified!

If the living conditions left a little to be desired, what about the rest of the school?

For a start, the small iron gates that were dotted at various intervals around the outer wall. These were always padlocked to keep any unwanted people from gaining access to the grounds. The children, though, were sure that the real intention was to keep *them* from getting out.

And what about those well-equipped classrooms? The extortionate fees charged by the school had paid for all these marvellous resources. Surely they were enough to satisfy everyone's needs? Well, no, actually, because the children were hardly ever allowed to use them. This equipment was all for show!

It was a strictly enforced rule, announced by the Headmaster, Godfrey Randolph Mannering, that "the school's facilities must never under any circumstances be touched by any grubby paw of any grubby child." No working on computers, no experimenting with the scientific apparatus, no swimming in the heated pools and definitely no reading in, or even entering, the New Library at any time whatsoever. There was just one exception – on Open Days, when parents were around to watch.

So, how did West Mayling children learn? Not, sadly, by using any of this smart modern equipment! No, they had to settle for all the old stuff – dusty Maths textbooks full of sum after sum written by old, even dustier, Oxford Professors; dog-eared copies of Shakespeare's 'Macbeth' or 'A Midsummer Night's Dream' with pages missing everywhere; cracked test tubes for Chemistry and powdered chemicals that were stuck together because tops didn't fit on their jars; glockenspiels with the 'C' note tuned like 'F sharp' and recorders sounding more like giraffes breaking wind than a well-oiled orchestra in full swing. To top it all, ovens from Victorian times that burnt everything within them to a cinder. All in all, it was a thoroughly disastrous show and, after a short while at school, students got pretty fed up.

Only two things kept them learning. First was their natural quest for knowledge and self-improvement. The second was a very weird phenomenon indeed – West Mayling's ubiquitous 'Code of Silence'.

The Code of Silence was a form of intimidation which emanated directly from the Head. It cast its web over everyone at West Mayling House – the children and the staff. This was strange because Godfrey Mannering did not seem to be a dominant figure. He never yelled at anyone. He didn't rule the school with an 'iron fist'. Nor did he ever mention publicly that if anyone, child *or* teacher, broke the Code of Silence, then they would be in for the chop. But a powerful myth had developed that Godfrey Mannering had some *extremely* influential friends. And this menacing bunch had the power to make your life utterly miserable. Forever.

This was enough to send the appropriate shivers down the spine of any teacher who stepped out of line, or scare the living daylights out of any child who decided to 'try it on'. There were even rumours that children had been summoned to his Office, never to return or be seen again. Whether such rumours were true or not was neither here nor there. It was simply whispered from each child, year after year, that you kept your mouth shut and just put up with it.

One thing they did know for certain was that Godfrey Randolph Mannering had absolutely no time at all for children. He never acknowledged them, preferring to stay out of their way at all possible times. He always had a look of disgust on his face when they passed him in a corridor. He'd stand there with a pained expression, as if he'd rather be somewhere else. He obviously didn't relish working with children in any shape or form.

How did Mannering maintain this Code of Silence? Well, he always employed teachers who had 'secrets' in their past about which they preferred to keep quiet. And he always had something up his sleeve that he could use to blackmail the children.

For example, Arthur Malcolm Cuthbertson, the Science Teacher. Cuthbertson enjoyed more than the odd tipple of Scotch. As a result, his teaching wasn't always up to scratch. His lowest point occurred when he fell asleep during one of his experiments with the Second Form, knocking over a vat of pure sulphuric acid. The acid ate its way through his desk, the floor, cables and drains, polluting the soil below for about fifteen years. The Headmaster gently reminded him of this whenever Cuthbertson commented on the state of the Science resources or on his lowly salary. He soon returned sheepishly to his duties.

Similarly with the Latin Teacher, 'Dusty' Clive Shaw. The Headmaster found out that Shaw once had a reputation for 'petty acquisition'. During a mad spree at College, he was said to have taken anything from bubble-gum to ladies' hats and scarves. The Head brought this up every time Dusty Shaw got hot under the collar about something that bothered him. He certainly failed to 'veni, vidi, vici' in *his* meetings with the Head!

The children were amazed at how he had got to know about all of their bad habits. For example, 'Fatty' Balshaw's secret binges with school chocolate, always locked up in the Kitchens, were discovered by the Headmaster. Fatty was held to ransom on this point should he ever appear to break the Code. The Head found out about Anthony Lincetti's secret gambling sessions. 'Big' Tony Lincetti was under the legal age to gamble and Mannering told him "You could face criminal prosecution, Lincetti, if this information was released to the Press." That would have ruined the reputation of his Italian father, Alessandro Lincetti, a prominent Judge at The Old Bailey in London.

Worst of all was young 'Blankets' McDougal. His unfortunate nickname was picked up during his first few days at West Mayling when he couldn't control his bladder at night. He was under threat that his little secret might be "published on the Notice Board" if he ever caused any trouble. 'Blankets' had no choice. He didn't want that difficulty from his past on display.

These tactics of intimidation hung over just about everybody in the school, from the Teaching Staff to the children, from Ground Staff even to the milkman, who delivered each Tuesday and Thursday morning.

Fortunately, there *was* one exception.

Arty Fox.

He was the only person whom Godfrey had missed, so he had nothing hanging around his neck like a hangman's noose. This is why he became the one to rebel, the reason why the Headmaster's influence and power eventually crumbled and fell.

As you are now about to find out...

Chapter 3

The Rumble In The Jungle

The rumble in the jungle began on a boring Thursday afternoon. It was three fifty-five, only five minutes to go before the bell signalled the end of yet another fruitless day and the beginning of another fruitless evening. Homework consisted of a French translation, twenty Science questions on the life-cycle of a frog and an English poem to be read. Then there was a technical drawing to complete: a three-dimensional design for a 'new' pencil sharpener. Arty wanted to design something more appropriate like a homework-writing robot or an alarm clock that rang every time he nodded off. With the painful drudgery of all this work ahead of him, he knew that he would certainly need *something* to keep him awake.

The great school bell rang. A murmured cheer came from all who were present in Dr Reynolds' Maths lesson. Dr Rupert J Reynolds resented the implication that his Maths lesson had been of a boring nature. He proceeded to prescribe "the cure for cheekiness" – as he put it – by assigning everyone fifty division sums as extra homework. A groan of disapproval greeted this announcement, so the fifty was raised sharply to seventy-five.

Arty shook his head and slowly exhaled a deep sigh of disbelief. He brushed his hand through his blonde hair, piled his books into his bag and swung it around on to his shoulder. Head down, he followed his closest mates, Cyril 'Sid' Gumbar, Jimmy 'Brains' Mahoy and Sophie 'Soppy' Burns out of the classroom, not daring to whisper anything in case the sums were increased to a nice, round one hundred. As soon as they entered the corridor, Arty turned round to Brains.

"Can you believe 'The Bear' did that?" he groaned.

They called Dr Reynolds 'The Bear' because of his first name, Rupert. They'd found it out when they were First Formers, so Rupert 'The Bear' Reynolds it became.

"Well, as a matter of fact, yes, I can, Arty," replied Brains, tilting his head down and looking at him above his glasses. "The Bear did that to us twice last week and once the week before that. Also, if I'm not mistaken – which I very rarely am – young Palmer in the First Form mentioned they got fifty of his 'finest' a day or two ago."

"Yeah, come off it, Arty," interrupted Soppy, "don't tell me you're that surprised! The Bear's a grumpy old beggar at this time of year. It's because he's just come out of hibernation!"

"I'd say he needs to get out a bit more often!" remarked Arty sarcastically. "Might help him realise that there happens to be a whole world out there apart from algebra, fractions and that awful rubbish from Pythagoras!"

"Ah, Pythagoras!" sighed Sid, breathing in deeply. "One of the 'Wonders of the World'! Where would our civilisation be without the brilliance of Pythagoras?"

"A damn sight more happy!" answered Arty, talking to himself more than to the others.

"Ah, no! I can't let that pass, Mr Fox!" announced Sid jokingly. "I can't let you smear the good name of Pythagoras without standing up and defending him!"

"Yeah? Well, go on then, Sid, do your worst!"

"Right, for a start, his Theorem is... well, it's a true art... a... sophisticated system." Sid looked up in the air and then at the other three, who just stood there smiling. "OK, so it's a pile of pants! So, what's next on our thrilling list of 'World Important Issues' to discuss?"

"Not your pants, I can assure you!" giggled Soppy. "I couldn't think of anything I'd rather not talk about than your pants, Sid!"

"Hey, you should count yourself lucky, Sops," grinned Arty. "You don't have to see him wandering around in them!"

"Hmmm!" exclaimed Brains. "Nor do you have to endure seeing them lying on your carpet while he's taking a wash."

"Nor witness, when he washes, the backside that graces the inside of them!" blurted Arty.

"Oh, Arty!" scoffed Soppy, in joint disgust and laughter. "Trust you!"

"Er... do you think that we could halt the discussions about my backside, my pants and any other personal possessions of mine, please?" requested Sid, a little rosy-cheeked and flushed. Although he had now known Soppy for three years he still felt a bit embarrassed by a discussion like this in front of her. "Could we focus for just a moment on the gruelling task that awaits us tonight? Do you remember? The small task of all this homework."

That put the dampers on the frivolity and brought them back to reality with a bump. The smiles departed and the groans returned. Their faces became a picture. This picture said a thousand words – like 'depression', 'dread' and 'anguish' – with 'misery', 'rejection' and 'disbelief' thrown in for good measure.

They ambled along the corridor, out through the Maths Block and over the courtyard to the Main Buildings. Then they went upstairs to the Old Library where they always did their homework.

Being Third Formers they could have gone back to their rooms. This, though, would have left Soppy on her own, as the girls and the boys were kept strictly apart in their rooms. These four, whatever they decided to do, always stayed as a team.

So, what can be said about these four friends?

Well, Arty had the appearance of a surfer... blonde hair, blue eyes, tanned skin and a winning smile. In Arty's presence, lots of girls would go weak at the knees. Arty, though, was not one to boast – he never rated his looks. He always stated that he was simply 'plain and ordinary'. However, because of his drive, his charisma and his sense of duty and fairness, he'd become a bit of an idol.

Soppy was every bit Arty's match. She was a pretty girl, with her long dark hair and hazel-brown eyes which sparkled when she smiled. Soppy was intelligent, sharp and sensitive. She was admired and respected by everyone.

Sid was the whingeing comic of the group. The quiet one – with scruffy black hair, a scruffy black rucksack, totally disorganised and an odd sense of humour. His ill-timed, one-line gags amused only Arty. But the others loved and cared for him nevertheless. Sid was innocent and harmless – they all knew he was absolutely loyal.

Brains was the genius of West Mayling House. With his thin frame and freckles, his round, black-rimmed spectacles and his floppy, black, centre-parted hair, he looked like your typical 'Teckie'. Everyone held him in high esteem. Incredibly knowledgeable, astute, a stickler for detail, Brains was a very serious planner.

Even though they came from different feeder Prep Schools, they'd hit it off immediately. Ever since the First Form at West Mayling they'd been firm friends.

If someone was stuck, everyone would help. If one was behind with homework, the others would gee them on. If one had a problem or felt upset, they'd rally round to assist. No matter what, no matter when, no matter if it conflicted with their own plans, the team always came first. It was an unwritten rule, part of a pact they'd agreed on soon after starting at school.

It was strange how they met and immediately liked each other. In the early days, the boys got some 'ribbing' from the others who saw they'd made such close friends with a girl. But, to the boys, Soppy was as good a mate as the other three. Although she'd received a bit of an ear-bashing from her girlfriends, Soppy really appreciated their friendship.

Seeing how strong a team they'd become, other First Form boys and girls called them the 'Four Musketeers'. The others even began to talk to one another much more readily. Over time, this all resulted in a Third Form that got on really well. There was, of course, the occasional clash between a girl and a boy, but this had never arisen between these four friends. What's more, it never looked likely to happen. It was this friendship and the immense trust between these friends that enabled the rebellion to become a reality and to last the distance.

As you are about to find out...

* * *

That evening, the Four Musketeers chipped away at their homework until it was nearly time for lights out. The boys said their "good-nights" to Soppy and returned to the room they shared with three others –

Big Tony Lincetti, Fatty Balshaw and Mitch McGovern.

What can we say about these three friends?

Well, Big Tony was the entrepreneur of the seven. Anything that made money interested him. Born in Palermo, in Sicily, he had all the looks of an over-fed, Italian footballer... black hair, blue eyes and olive-brown, silky skin. But he liked his pasta so his tall frame was well-padded – particularly around the waist.

Fatty was even more padded! Strawberry-blonde, tall and pear-shaped he was forever in good spirits, always introducing *himself* as 'Fatty' Balshaw! Rosy-cheeked, with a jovial round face, he had a heart of gold. Ever smiling, he was well-liked by everyone – for his humour, his patience, his loyalty and good nature.

Mitch was the tallest of them all. Athletic, muscular and hailed as the sporting idol – he was captain of every School Team. He liked his mousy hair cropped closely, his chin freshly shaven and his clothes smart and respectable. He was an ideal advertisement for West Mayling House.

These six boys became really good mates. They'd established a set of rules for the room that seemed fair and decent and set up a rota for their cleaning duties. This meant they were never caught out by the teacher in charge for having an untidy room, so they wouldn't lose any precious free time at weekends.

Chores for children having messy rooms included cleaning the staff toilets, washing their cars, ironing their linen, cutting the courtyard grass with a pair of scissors or even digging the Headmaster's cabbage patch on the school allotment. They'd all suffered these early on in the First Form. So they decided that, in the Third Form, when they could choose who shared their room, they would set up a proper system.

With the friendship between the three boys and Soppy and the special relationship of the six mates in this room, you can see that the West Mayling Third Form was a pretty tight bunch!

After the routine of washing and getting ready for bed had been accomplished – which, with six people sharing one basin, took remarkable coolness and patience – they all turned themselves into their beds to start their nightly 'chat session'.

"Tony, it would make a change if we could enjoy a 'fragrance-free' night tonight!" smirked Fatty.

"Blimey, that's rich coming from you, Fats!" retorted Tony, laughing. "I'm not the one who eats a double helping of eggs and beans for lunch then polishes off *four* of my mates' jam sponge with custard!"

"Yes, Fatty," added Mitch. "Where do you put it all, pal?"

"I dare say that there's plenty of storage space in your immense digestive system, eh, Fatty?" suggested Brains.

"Oh, yes!" answered Fatty, patting his belly as it cast a curved silhouette against the light that shone in through the window. "Plenty of room down below, young Mahoy!"

"Then maybe it could all stay *there* tonight," chuckled Big Tony, "rather than being reprocessed and expelled through your flabby cheeks!"

"Girls, girls, please!" interrupted Arty sarcastically. "Even though I would also appreciate our room being an odour-free zone, could we turn our attention to something that's a little more thought-provoking?"

"Like what?" asked Sid.

"Like all that laughter I can hear in the distance."

"What laughter?" asked Sid. "I can't hear anything, can you, guys?"

"That's because you're gassing on about Fatty's bowels!" exclaimed Arty. "Just button it – and listen."

All six boys stopped chatting and pricked up their ears, trying to hear the laughter that Arty claimed was outside. The window was open, allowing the cool, clear, Spring air to circulate through the room. The six boys had always kept the window open, usually because Fatty's eating habits created a desperate need for fresh air. But now they were on the *fourth* floor, they could also hear anything that was going on within the school grounds.

For the last few nights Arty swore he'd heard the sound of laughter and light music wafting its way through the air. He hadn't paid too much attention to it at first but, as it was clearly much more distinct that night, he'd brought it to the others' notice.

"You're right, Arty. That's definitely the sound of laughter," whispered Brains.

"Yes, I heard it as well."

"Me, too."

"So where's it coming from?" asked Sid.

"I reckon the Staffroom," suggested Fatty.

"Yes... could be... although I think it's from Godfrey's room," answered Arty.

"No way!"

"Never!"

"I have to agree, Arty," said Brains. "It does seem highly unlikely that any laughter would be coming from 'God' himself. He's not exactly that sort of person is he?"

The 'God' they were referring to was, of course, the Headmaster, Godfrey Randolph Mannering. Because he so dominated the school without seeming to be a monster, they'd chosen a perfect nickname. They'd shortened 'Godfrey' to 'God'. This suited his image of total control, of being omniscient, omnipotent and omnipresent.

"No, I'm telling you, that is *definitely* the sound of more than one person laughing. I'm equally as sure that it's coming from either his room or the Staffroom," insisted Arty.

The boys listened carefully and heard more sounds of laughter. This time it was evident that women as well as men were involved. Arty sat up in bed and looked over at his alarm clock. It read 11:17.

Far too late for a party to be held at West Mayling. Surely?

Chapter 4

Secrets

"Right. That's it!" whispered Arty. "I'm going to investigate. This must be the tenth night I've heard these party noises. I *have* to find out what's going on!"

"Hey, steady, Arty!" exclaimed Sid. "You don't want to get caught, you know. It's far too dangerous to go off at this time of night."

"Yes, come on, Arty," added Mitch. "Sid is right. There's no way you'd make it down there without getting caught."

"Then we'd all get the can thrown at us!" said Tony.

"Oh, come off it, girls," continued Arty. "Where's your sense of adventure? I mean, just how much trouble can we get into? It's not like we're staying in some kind of army camp, is it?"

"Yes it is!"

"Yes."

"Yep!"

"It is, too!"

"Course it is," said Sid. "We all know it feels like a bloomin' army camp round here – and that's just on the good days!"

"Yeah. OK. This school *is* like an army camp. I still say that we go and investigate. I want to know who these 'happy people' are and who's having all the fun. It doesn't sound like *they're* in a bloomin' army camp!" That made the others think.

"OK. I'm in!" started Mitch.

"Yeah, me too," added Fatty.

"I'm there!" whispered Big Tony.

"If I absolutely must!" sighed Sid.

"Yes, I ditto that. Only if I absolutely must," said Brains, "and I want it noted for the record that I think it's a mistake. When we're caught, let it not be said that I didn't tell you so!"

"Thank you, Mum," concluded Arty. "We'll make a note of your concerns. But, despite all this, I still say we go for it anyway!"

As they were about to set out on their undercover mission to discover who was having such fun – because it certainly wasn't them – Brains stopped them again.

"Arty?

"What is it, Brains?"

"Can I just ask you something?"

"Yeah, sure."

"What's actually bugging you so suddenly?"

"I don't really know," started Arty, thinking hard about the question. "I can't quite put my finger on it, only I feel that somebody's up to something. It's really beginning to bother me."

"What is?"

"I don't know, Brains, I just don't know. I feel kind of fed up. I do begrudge people who seem to be having such fun when we're missing out. You guys must feel the same, surely?"

"I do," admitted Mitch.

"Yeah, me too," agreed Big Tony, "but I keep on telling myself just to ignore it, you know... because of all the trouble it might bring?"

"Yes, OK, so there could be trouble," continued Arty, "but sometimes you've got to take a stand."

"Not necessarily, Arty!" said Sid. "Not if you have to face God because of it!"

"Alright, so you might have to face God, but..."

"That's bad enough!" yelped Sid. "That's enough of a deterrent to stop me from taking a stand, I can tell you!"

"Sid, a pink poodle with a high-pitched yelp would deter you from climbing over a fence. I hardly think your measure of bravery is something I should lead my life by."

"Arty?"

"What?"

"Bite me."

"Oh, come on, Sid, I just feel differently at the moment, that's all. I want to go and investigate this laughter. Don't get me wrong, I don't want to get any of you into trouble." Arty looked around the room at the boys' half-lit faces.

"I just think... we owe it to ourselves."

That statement was a definitive point. It was the moment that a spark of rebellion was ignited in the others. It summed up, then changed how they thought. There they were – young, carefree, at the prime of life but they *knew* they should feel much happier in school than they were. Arty's words inspired a sense of duty within them. Not only did they *owe* it to themselves to improve their situation, it was down to each one of them to *do* something about it. Now they were united. Now they were determined to act.

Arty put his slippers and dressing gown on first and crouched down by the dormitory door. He peered back at the others. They were copying him, still with looks of trepidation. When the six were dressed and ready, Arty gave the 'thumbs up'. He slowly opened the bedroom door and crept out on to the landing. The others followed closely. They ventured cautiously along the corridor towards the four flights of stairs which led down to the Staffroom. Every step they took needed to be as silent as possible because to be caught would carry a hefty penalty.

Everything seemed fine until Fatty accidentally dropped a sweet-wrapper and trod on it. The wrinkled paper crunched under his slipper and echoed around the landing. The other five turned and glared at him as the eerie silence was broken. Their movements may have been heard. Fatty screwed up his face, realising that he had blundered badly and held up his hand to apologise. As he did so, the door to the room they were passing opened and Alex Barnes poked out his head.

"Bonjourno, gentlemen!" he said with a curious smile on his face.

"Go back to bed please, Barnsey!" whispered Arty Fox forcibly. "Forget you ever saw us here, OK?"

"Oh! Feisty, aren't we? So what's 'Farty Sox' and his room-mates doing out here at this time of night? Going on a jaunt, are we?"

"Put a sock in it, Barnsey!" hissed Mitch.

"If you get caught, you know that –"

"But," snapped Sid, "we won't get caught, will we, Barnsey. Because you didn't see anything, did you?"

"Well, that depends. What's it worth?"

"Barnsey," interrupted Arty, "if you don't creep back into that little shell of yours, I'll get Mitch here to hang you up from the clock-tower by your Y-fronts. Now!"

Barnsey knew his place. He withdrew his head meekly and shut the door. Arty turned round to the others with an expression of 'that was a close one'. Brains raised his eyebrows, as if to say "I knew this was going to happen." Sid held his hand on his chest, feeling every thumping pulse from his racing heart. Arty took a deep breath and waved them forward. They crept along the rest of the corridor and carefully descended the stairs.

As they reached the second floor, the noises from below were even more audible – loud enough for some of the First Formers to have heard. Arty thought that it may have caused some of them to stir, even come to the door to see who it was. But he knew the First Formers were more easily scared of doing such things. Only the bravest of the brave or the stupidest of the stupid would have come to check what was going on.

The six boys continued on down, past the First Floor, listening intently to the sounds that came from the general direction of the Staffroom. They heard music playing in the background, then the sporadic sound of giggles followed by bursts of more rapturous laughter. Every time these outbursts occurred, the six would freeze and look round at each other with bemused smirks, eyebrows raised and furrowed foreheads.

"What's going on?"

"Who is it?"

Arty gestured for the others to follow him.

He moved off the staircase and tiptoed across the Entrance Hall. He crept through Devinia's room and finally stopped just outside the Headmaster's Office. Bending down, he placed his ear close to the keyhole.

He definitely heard the Head's voice, apparently telling a joke. When he spoke there was silence. When he stopped, lots of laughter. This seemed very strange to Arty. He'd never had a hate complex against Godfrey Mannering, mainly because he'd never crossed his path. Nor had he ever seen

Mannering bellow at anyone in public, so he knew that the Head was not a fierce 'dragon-like' creature breathing fire over everyone. Conversely, because he hadn't ever seen him smile or show a glimmer of humour in his facial expressions, it felt extremely odd to hear the Head in such good spirits and talking so freely and happily.

Although Arty couldn't make out exactly what Mannering said, he managed to grasp the odd word. Much more difficult were the other voices – whose were they? Arty looked back at his room-mates and mimed the words "Is that the staff?"

Mitch shrugged his shoulders. So did Big Tony. But Brains acknowledged Arty's thoughts with a 'thumbs up'. Arty gestured that they should follow him and then crept back along the Hall towards the back Kitchen.

"Was that the staff I could hear in God's room?" asked Arty.

"Well, I thought it was," replied Brains.

"That's crazy!" retorted Sid in a surprised whisper. "It's almost half-eleven. What are the staff still doing in his room at this time of night?"

"Boozing, by the sounds of it!" hissed Fatty. "I definitely heard a hiccup and some giggles!"

Arty was intrigued by the situation. He wanted to find out more. He signalled to the others and headed for the Front Door.

"Now where are we going?" asked Fatty.

"To get a better view!" answered Arty.

Arty and Brains looked at each other and thought for a while. They knew this was another crucial step in their escapade. From here on there was no turning back. If they ventured through the Front Door, they were risking 'capture'. If they were found outside at night, they were certainly in for the chop. They knew it. The other four knew it, too. Anxiety was running high amongst the group. Brains raised his eyebrow one final time. Arty winked at him and nodded his head. That meant... they continued.

Brains crouched by the heavy oak door and took a pair of tweezers out of his dressing gown. He slotted them into the lock and started to turn them to the left and right. The other boys looked nervously around the Entrance Hall, praying that no-one could hear what Brains was up to. With one final turn Brains succeeded in unlocking the door. He opened it slowly. Sid cringed with every creak of the hinges. He closed his eyes and swallowed hard. Once the door was ajar, Arty crept through. The others followed him outside into the cool, Spring air.

The moon was full and it cast a glorious, bright, silver light across the whole landscape. An owl hooted in one of the great oaks in the grounds. Sid stopped abruptly. He turned round to check who it was.

No-one. Phew! Relief.

The group continued along the edge of the grass, avoiding the gravelled pathway, until they reached the huge window at the back of the Head's Office.

The large, crimson curtains were drawn but, luckily, not fully. There was a slight gap between the bottom of the curtains and the top of the radiator. The window was slightly open and the voices could be heard much more clearly than in the Entrance Hall. The first voice to speak was a foreign one.

"I must congratulate you, Monsieur Mannering, on your fine choice of wine!"

"That's Philippe Saint-Moreaux," whispered Brains, "the French Teacher."

"I thank you, Philippe," came the Head's voice in reply. "It's a Taittinger Comtes de Champagne – Blanc de Blancs – 1988. Vintage, don't you know. One of the finest you can buy."

"Eeze eet expensive, Monsieur?"

"But of course, Philippe! It costs over three hundred pounds a bottle! But after our little 'business venture', I'm sure we'll be able to drink this and nothing else from now on."

"Business venture?" whispered Sid. "What's he talking about?"

"Beats me," replied Arty. "Let's listen a bit more."

"Oh, Headmaster, I have to hand it to you. You've certainly got an eye for the good life!"

"That's Devinia Longchamps, God's Secretary!" whispered Brains.

"Oh yes, Devinia," continued the Head. "I said all those years ago that, if you stuck with me and kept the Code of Silence, we'd all benefit in the end."

"So how much do you think we'll have altogether, Headmaster?"

"And that's Dickie Howard, our English Teacher!" announced Brains, feeling he was reeling off a 'Who's Who' list of the staff.

"Well, Dr Reynolds is the mathematician with all the figures, Dickie. He's informed me that by the end of this academic year we'll have amassed just over one and a half million pounds! This will leave us close to fifty thousand to party with until the end of the Summer Term. Not bad, is it?"

"Oh, Headmaster, you're an absolute genius, Sir!"

"That's Wellington Waters, the History Teacher!" hissed Brains again.

"Never mind old 'Wellie'," urged Big Tony. "What about that million and a half? What on earth does he mean by that? Where is he getting it from?"

"Thank you, Wellington," continued the Head. "Yes, I have to admit that I am rather chuffed with my Scheme."

"Hmmm, yes, all those lovely rich parents, eh, Headmaster? If only they knew where their money was really going!"

"That's Sebastian Bannister, the Sports Teacher!" hissed Brains.

"Brains!" interrupted Arty. "We all know who they are, because we all have them too, remember? So concentrate on what they're saying rather than on who's talking!"

"Yeah, so what was all that about our parents?" asked Fatty.

"Well, I have to correct you there, Sebastian," advised the Head. "Granted, my brother in London has invested our money in stocks and shares, foreign currency and other clever schemes. But we *are* buying *some* school resources with a *little* of the profits we've made... you know, enough to keep up appearances! As long as we keep those blessed kids off the equipment so it stays clean and intact, we won't have to spend much more of it. We can therefore keep most of the money for our 'Early Retirement Scheme'. I can't see what's wrong with that. It's we who are using our brains. We're making that money work twice as hard as it would do if it just sat in an *ordinary* bank. What if we're using a little of the fee money for ourselves? We've still managed to buy the new computer suite, build the New Library and Sports Hall and get all this damned expensive technology. What more do they want? Besides, we hard-working teachers deserve a few 'perks', do we not?"

That generated a huge laugh from the delighted teachers. They all gave a cheer of approval as they lolled around on the furniture inside the Head's Office. The boys heard glasses clinking together in a toast and the guzzling sound of merry adults celebrating a bit too much! Arty was amazed by what he'd just heard. The jaws of the others were wide open. Their eyes bulged far enough to fall out of their sockets.

"He's embezzling our money!" hissed Brains. "No wonder we can never use any of this new equipment! It's all for show! It's all to keep the parents quiet and stop them asking questions! It all has to stay clean and tidy so the Head doesn't have to buy any more!"

"So... they invest the school's money in stocks and shares and the like," whispered Arty, holding his palm flat against his forehead. "They use a little bit of the profit to buy some school equipment. But all the rest goes into... *retirement* nest-eggs for themselves?"

"Well, that actually sounds rather brilliant to me!" exclaimed Big Tony. The others all looked at him out of the corners of their eyes. "Well it does," he continued. "It's ingenious. And it's great business!"

"Tony, it's a scam!" replied Brains. "It may be clever but it must be illegal. They're charging fees – which are far too high – and they're only using a tiny amount of it to run the school. The rest is literally lining their pockets. We're not seeing a whiff of it! We don't even benefit from the resources that we *have* got here."

"So, what are you saying, Brains?" asked Sid.

"Hello! Anybody at home, Sid?" Brains groaned sarcastically. "Sid. Think about it. If all the fee money was used properly, West Mayling would be the best school in the country! We could even afford to have... a music studio... a new theatre with the latest hi-tech lighting and sound. Perhaps two or three specialist libraries... ones we can actually use!"

"So, what are you saying, Brains?" repeated Sid.

"What?"

"Unfortunately, I have to agree with Sid," added Tony. "Just what are we supposed to do with all this knowledge, now that we know it?"

"Well, we've got to do something. Right, Arty?" Brains turned to Arty for support. Arty sat motionless, looking up at the heavens, not really listening to anyone.

"Yes, Brains, we've got to do something. And I know what I'm going to do..."

Arty stood up. Without uttering a word, he started to walk casually back along the grass. He didn't bother to crouch down to avoid being seen but strode straight towards the Front Door. He paused and turned his body half round. He glanced at the others who sat watching him, bemused by his sudden departure. He beckoned for them to follow and returned to the Entrance Hall. Brains, attending to detail as ever, carefully locked the Front Door with his tweezers.

On the way back the others took turns to ask Arty questions. What was he thinking? Why were they returning to their room? Why now?

Arty didn't answer. He simply put his finger over his lips as a sign for them to keep quiet and smiled at each of them in turn. When they eventually arrived, they sat on the edge of their beds and eagerly awaited his answer.

So, why were they especially interested in Arty's ideas? Why were his ideas so significant?

Arty Fox was a good friend – and a trusted one at that. Apart from his good looks, his crystal blue eyes and his blonde hair, he was very smart, very quick-witted. Like Soppy, Arty seemed to be able to view every situation truly, fully, sensibly, without being over-emotional. In fact, that was why Arty and Soppy had become such good friends – they both thought in the same kind of way.

Don't get the wrong picture here, though. The others were clever, astute boys, who were all great friends. However, each boy had a tendency to do things or think in their own particular way. They had good ideas, which they did follow through from time to time. But they all agreed that it was Arty's opinion that carried the weight.

That was why, at eleven fifty-nine on that Thursday night, the five boys were so keen to hear what Arty was thinking.

"Girls," started Arty in a quiet voice, "I think that the puzzling feeling I've had recently has been answered. I felt that something bizarre was going on with all that laughter, though I never expected it to be anything like this!"

"So, what are you saying?" chirped Sid.

"Girls, this just isn't cricket!" continued Arty. "As I see it, they're making fools of us. Those teachers are pulling the wool over our eyes and our parents' eyes, too. We're being swindled. We're being swindled and robbed! Well, I'm not standing for it any more!"

"So, what are you saying?" asked Sid again.

"I'm saying *I've* had enough, Sid. I'm tired of being at the blunt end of the stick. I've had enough of using duff old equipment when there's perfectly good stuff around. I'm sick of the ridiculous amount of mind-destroying homework set by those teachers. And as for Godfrey's Code of Silence – that's just got to be broken!"

"If we break that Code, we're all going to suffer," urged Brains. "God's got a hold over us all."

"And now we know why! He's got a grip over *us* so *he* can swindle the school *and* get away with it. Take yourself, for instance, Brains. When we sneaked out to the Race Course last Summer, you picked the locks of the gates. Godfrey found out. Now, if you break the Silence, you'll be thrown out on that charge.

Fatty here is under threat for pinching Cook's chocolate and Tony for gambling. You're in trouble, Sid, because you accidentally found last year's exam papers. God's branded you a "cheat" – which is totally untrue – but you can't prove it, can you? Then there's Mitch, for that tackle in the rugby game last year. OK, poor Smithy did break his leg. But forgive me if I'm wrong, isn't rugby a contact sport? Anyway, God threatens Mitch with "assault and bodily harm" though it's all nonsense. Don't you see? He's got you all."

He paused.

"But... he hasn't got me. There's *no* threat hanging over me."

"How come, Arty?"

"I don't know, it's just never happened. We've never crossed paths. I'm probably the only person in this school who's slipped through his iron grip of power. My guess is he's lost my name. I'm not on any of his lists!"

"So, what are you saying?" Sid repeated.

"I'm much less afraid of the Code of Silence," smiled Arty. "In fact, I've now got something to hold over God and all his little 'disciples'. Embezzling the school funds and illegal stock investment! I'd say that's worth at least twenty years hard labour if anyone gets to hear about it."

"So, what are you saying?" asked Sid, yet again.

"Are those your favourite words tonight, Sid?"

"Come on, Arty! I'm serious! What are you saying?"

Arty looked at his five friends. He smiled.

"I'll tell you what I'm saying. I say: we rebel!"

Chapter 5

Chinese Whispers

As Friday dawned and the morning mist hung low over the fields, shrouding the landscape for miles around under a vast, light grey blanket, plans were already afoot for the first phase of the revolution.

The rebellious intentions, to which Arty had given birth on the previous night, had kept the other five members of the group wide awake. If Arty meant what he said – which they were certain he did – then talk of revolution would turn to reality. An unprecedented, historical and *terrifying* prospect!

The morning saw the six of them keeping deadly quiet, in a daydream, their minds miles away from any schoolwork placed in front of them. Ideas were whirling around inside their heads as each came to terms with the commitment they had made.

Arty told Soppy that the group had to meet. Time: twelve o'clock. Venue: under the great oak tree at the far end of the Hockey Pitch. Reason: there was a very urgent matter they needed to discuss.

Lunchtime came and the seven students made their way to the oak tree. Once there, they checked to make sure that no unwanted persons were in the vicinity or could overhear their conversation. Only the reclusive Art Teacher, Paul 'Pablo' Durrant, could be seen. He was lost in his own little world – sketching the Spring flowers on display in the school grounds – but too far away to pick up their voices.

Arty described to Soppy what they witnessed the night before. He told her about the music and the laughter. He told her about the journey downstairs and outside. He told her about the party and what they discovered about Godfrey's scheme with the money.

Soppy listened carefully. Was he pulling her leg – again? She looked at each of them in turn, trying to fathom out if this were some kind of joke. After a while, though, she realised that the boys were utterly serious.

At that point, Arty told her about *their* decision...

"Sops, you know Arty wouldn't come up with an idea that hadn't been completely thought through," started Brains.

"Yes... And...?"

"Well, we're all totally agreed on this. We feel we'd be acting with just cause and reason. We intend to go forward with this rebellion."

"And?"

"We need your support."

"*My* support?" Soppy choked. "For a revolt against the Headmaster and the teachers?"

"Yes," confirmed Brains, "because we need the girls behind us. We won't win without them."

"Too right you won't."

"Absolutely... yes. So, obviously... ummm... that's where you come in."

"I *see*. You want *me* to rally round all my girlfriends, then get *them* to rally round theirs, and to all join together to follow Arthur James Fox into some hair-brained scheme that includes revolting against the teachers? All because *you* think they've nicked a little bit of *our* money?"

"Yesss..."

Silence.

"OK! When do we start?"

Arty blew a sigh of relief. "Phew... thanks, Sops."

"No probs, Arty."

"And thanks for keeping us in suspense like that!"

Soppy smiled like a Cheshire cat. "Any time, Arty!"

* * *

Brains got their attention back. He reminded them of the need to come up with a very good, very thorough plan, very quickly, if they were going to have any success at all.

"Come on, fellows. Think! Think!" he said urgently. "We've only got fifty minutes left. If we're going to make use of this weekend to start things off, we must get cracking! We have to finalise some detailed plans. We need to enlist the support of all the others. We must get *everyone* behind us, otherwise our rebellion will fall flat on its face!"

"Brains, as usual, is completely right," announced Arty. "We must get the First and Second Forms on our side. But, first, we have to convince the Third Formers. Being the oldest and having younger brothers and sisters lower down the school, we can use them as sub-leaders. They can then direct their own troops to carry out our plans. The younger ones will look up to them and do as they're told. How's that for starters?"

"Agreed," replied the others in unison.

"Good. Right, this is what I have in mind..."

The seven huddled close together in a circle.

Arty explained his game plan. They discussed the general points and agreed their own personal tasks. Above all, Arty reminded them, they *must* stay united.

Well, the last point was never really in doubt, was it? The seven friends were such a strong team. Their total trust and respect for one another was the key element. It was – as you're about to see – the foundation that would inspire the others. It would give them the courage and the strength to ensure that the West Mayling rebellion would ultimately succeed.

* * *

That Friday became known as 'Chinese Whisper Day' due to all the secret preparations that took place during the afternoon. This is how things happened...

A mass meeting was going to be held in the Sports

Pavilion the next morning after Sports Practice. It was the ideal venue. Everyone who needed to attend would be there already, so it wouldn't look suspicious for so many pupils to be in one place at the same time.

Arty instructed the others to spread the word about this meeting through the Third, Second and First Forms that afternoon, a feat that was easier said than done.

Just before the start of lessons, each of the seven went to friends they knew well and told them to pass on the news. Only very trusted students were given this initial task. The rest would have to find out later.

During the lessons sheets of paper were secretly passed from hand to hand, under desks, across the backs of seats, folded into paper aeroplanes and guided from one corner of the room to the other. They were stuffed inside exercise books to be read out of sight of the teachers. On each slip of paper, it said:

'There is something rotten at West Mayling.
This is something only we can deal with.
Do you want your freedom?
Do you want to take control of your life?
Do you want a better school?

Meet in the Sports Pavilion at 12 noon Saturday.
This is not a request. It's an order!
Do not let us down and do not tell anyone.
Grassers will be dealt with severely!
Signed: Arty Fox'

Arty was taking a huge risk by actually putting his name to such an announcement, but he had insisted. Having his name on it, he said, guaranteed that it was genuine and could be trusted. Brains thought it was a very smart thing to do and heartily praised his friend for thinking of it. Arty said that they'd have to take risks on security because so many people had to be informed. This was something they'd simply have to put up with if the rebellion was going to get off the ground.

Surprisingly, security was not to be as big an issue as the seven had imagined. Although these bits of paper caused much curiosity and excitement, no-one let anything slip out of the bag.

Slowly but surely the word spread throughout the school. By the end of that Friday afternoon the first phase of the rebellion had been accomplished. Saturday's mass meeting had been set up. None of the teachers knew. All the children needed now was patience.

* * *

Saturday – at last. It had been an agonising wait from the end of school on Friday night to the finish of Sports Practice that morning. Everyone's performance that morning was lacklustre, to say the least. They were all thinking about the forthcoming meeting. The teachers in charge groaned and moaned about their "disappointing attitude" but none of the children took a blind bit of notice. Frustration and boredom were what they felt for the morning's tasks.

Sports Practice always started with a 'warm-up' – a five-mile run through the school grounds and local countryside. This included a pointless 'march' through the boggiest, soggiest and smelliest marshland just inside the grounds.

Pointless? Definitely.

Why?

Well, for one thing, the nature of a 'warm-up' should be to do just that – warm the body up – not kill it off before you've even started. Secondly, what was the point of wading through marshland with cold, stinking mud coming up to your knees? All it did, besides freezing your feet, was to cake your socks and boots completely in mud. This made running very difficult thereafter. Worse still, it took most of the afternoon to scrape your boots clean.

No-one ever figured out, either, why the teachers claimed that this run was "so good for you" or "so character-building" as Sebastian Bannister frequently proclaimed. None of them ever took part. If they were all so health conscious themselves, how come they *never* practised what they preached?

Anyway, nothing detracted from the same old routine: long distance run, followed by ball-handling skills and, finally, the 'big match'. Here, the whole school tucked in to a 'mass-bruising' session. Everyone always walked away from these rugby-like games completely battered, weary and totally dejected – not that it seemed to affect the teachers a jot.

However, on this particular Saturday, the thought of the secret meeting kept a spark alive. A 'buzz' was circulating around the grounds.

* * *

As the balls, cones and flags were collected and dragged back to the PE storerooms, the children made their way to the Sports Pavilion to shower and change. None of the teachers ever bothered to come into the Pavilion until a good hour after the practice sessions were complete. Then it was only to turf out any 'hangers-on' or 'slow-changers'. This was long enough for a meeting but it would still have to be well directed and concise to get through the main points in time. Brains had discussed these with Arty late on Friday.

Arty rehearsed the order of his speech throughout the night and even during Saturday morning's Sports Practice. He entered the Pavilion completely focussed, ready for the task in hand.

The Pavilion was a large square building that had wide concrete steps leading from the playing surface up to the front doors. Along the top steps were wooden benches for pupils to sit on and take off their boots before entering the building. To one side of these steps were the storerooms for all the sporting equipment. The inside of the Pavilion wasn't anything to write home about: dusty, damp, cold and pretty grubby all year round. It was never that nice to change in at any time. But, on this occasion, it was not the interior décor that had captured the minds of the pupils...

They entered the building and made for the largest of the damp wooden changing areas. A few Third Formers came in last after checking that no teachers were following them. Inside, the children congregated in groups. A desk had been placed at the front. Behind it sat Arty, flanked by Soppy and Brains, with Big Tony, Sid, Mitch and Fatty leaning against the window ledge. There wasn't really enough room for all three Forms in there but no-one was agitated by the cramped conditions. Everyone was concentrating entirely on the boy standing at the front.

That boy, of course, was Arty Fox.

* * *

"My Lords, Ladies and Gentlemen... Students... Friends. I have grave news to tell you," began Arty. "There is something distinctly rotten within West Mayling House!"

Whispered murmuring rippled round the room.

"Never, in the great history of our illustrious school, has such a travesty of justice been unearthed. Never, in the seven hundred and thirty-two years of this noble school, has such corruption, such unlawfulness, such downright cheek been shown!"

The audience gasped in shock. Some looked at their neighbours, others repeated some of Arty's words –

"Corruption?"

"Cheek?"

"Comrades, I urge you to listen very carefully to the words I'm about to say. Late on Thursday night my friends and I witnessed an unbelievable scene. God and the staff were discussing how they intend to spend this year's fee money."

Arty paused and stared round the room.

"Were they planning to drain the marshland that we wade through every Saturday morning? No. Were they planning to build a... slightly more decorative Pavilion? No. How about improving our dormitories? Giving us decent sheets? Comfortable beds? Perhaps, a basin each? No, not a word."

Another planned pause.

"Then surely it must be going on a music studio? No. What about the high-tech theatre we've all been talking about? Is that what they were discussing? No, definitely not!"

The audience was hooked in suspense. Why was Arty telling them this?

"Unfortunately, the truth is somewhat different. Money that should be spent on our school... on *you*...

is going directly into the teachers' pockets!"

The ranks of seated pupils stared aghast at Arty.

"They've got secret accounts. They're planning early retirement. *Very* early retirement – with massive unearned handouts! And they're using *our* money to fund it! It's a simple case of... embezzlement!"

Complete disbelief filled the Pavilion.

"What? No way!"

"Rubbish! *Can't* be true!"

Brains quickly realised that this reaction could be disastrous for the whole future of the rebellion. He knew that everyone *had* to believe Arty before anything more could be done. He stepped forward to address the crowd.

"Fellow West Mayling students, I understand how you might find this story very hard to accept. However, you're forgetting something! I hate to state the obvious, but the person standing before you and telling you these things is none other than... Arty Fox. It was Arty Fox's name that you saw on those pieces of paper yesterday, summoning you here today. You know what sort of person Arty Fox is. He's a man of principle, a man of values, of honesty and trust. You must listen closely to what he says – and you must have faith in him."

That did the trick very nicely. The pupils agreed wholeheartedly with Brains. The mood of the crowd turned completely.

"He's right!"

"It is Arty, after all"

"We must listen to him!"

Saved! Arty's presence and prestige were now restored. He continued.

"I know precisely how you feel. We, too, found it so difficult to believe. But it's true. It's all true. God is diverting a load of our money out of the school. Admittedly, he's bought a few new things over the past few years. But they're all for show. Think about it. Ask yourself this: Who's ever used those new PCs?"

The audience paused for thought.

"Have you swum in the heated swimming pools?"

The girls shook their heads.

"When were we last let into the New Library?"

Boys shook theirs.

"Exactly! I'll tell you when," exclaimed Arty. "Never! That's the one and only answer to these questions! Never!"

Nods of agreement came from the crowd.

"And why not? The reason is, God's very worried... that's why. He thinks we'll create a mess or spoil them. Heaven forbid if we ever broke anything! You see, God doesn't want to fork out any more money. He wants the lot for himself and his staff!"

It was definitely working. The room full of students now *heard* what Arty was saying. What's more, they agreed with him, too. As the truth slowly dawned, the mood changed again and they waved their arms in frustration.

Arty carried on.

"Now, ask yourself these questions: Why do we never complain to our parents? Why has this 'policy' never been challenged?"

He watched the blank expressions, the shrugging of shoulders.

"I'll tell you why. It's because of God's strategy of intimidation. He's threatened every single one of you about breaking the West Mayling Code of Silence!"

Eyes bulged wide. Arty looked round the room.

"Barnsey? Charlotte? Blankets? He's threatened you, hasn't he?"

They all nodded.

"And the rest of you?"

Realisation spread around the crowd. They saw just how plausible it all was and there weren't many present who were happy about it at all.

"Well, we've got the answer to this little *problem!*" continued Arty.

"Oooh!" grunted the crowd, now in the mood for solutions.

"We heard what we heard. We know what we know. We too can play Godfrey's little game. We've discovered his incredible secret. *We* can make it *public* if we want. Yes! That's *our* threat... with which *we* can pressure the Head!"

"Ahhh!" whispered the crowd.

"So, are we going to let Godfrey get away with this scandal?"

"Nooo..!" breathed the crowd, their excitement growing.

"And what about Godfrey's corruption? Is it right that he carries on in this shameful manner?"

"Nooo..!" they roared, driven on by Arty's words.

"How are we going to deal with all this?"

All faces were fixed upon Arty, eagerly awaiting the answer.

"How? I'll tell you how... with a *revolution!*"

The pupils let out an almighty cheer. So loud that it nearly blew out the changing room windows!

"We will revolt!" shouted Arty to yet another huge roar of approval from the others. *"We'll rebel!"* he cried.

A frenzied waving of arms, cheering and yelling, chanting and screaming followed. It seemed that the entire school had joined together as one huge army – disgruntled, though now inspired.

But not quite... it wasn't unanimous yet. Senior girls from the Third Form were talking seriously amongst themselves. The expression on their faces was far from enthusiastic. When the volume of cheering and chanting had calmed a little, one of them – Charlotte O'Driscoll – stood up and faced the front desk. A silence fell over the crowd.

"I... well... we here also feel unhappy about what's happening at West Mayling. But I want to know what Soppy has to say about the idea of rebellion. It's not that we aren't on your side or anything. It's just that we... like... want to hear a girl's perspective on the whole situation."

Charlotte sat down again. As Soppy stood up to respond, some First Form boys let out groans of disapproval. They thought it was soft not wanting to revolt against the teachers. Before Soppy could speak, Arty got up, placed a hand on her arm and addressed the audience first.

"Please – I don't want to hear anybody knocking anyone else's opinions," he said. "Everyone is entitled to have their full say. Everyone's thoughts will be respected. We have to work as a team if this revolution is to succeed. Help each other – both boys and girls – and we will win. Personally, I agree with Charlotte. We should hear what Soppy has to say."

Arty wanted to show publicly how he felt towards Soppy, who was as true a friend as Brains, Sid or any of the others. He wanted everyone to recognise that 'team spirit' was absolutely vital to the rebellion's success. Soppy smiled and stepped forward.

"I feel the same way as you, Charlie."

The First Form boys looked at each other and groaned. Typical girl, they thought. Even Charlotte O'Driscoll raised an eyebrow. Did she hear Soppy correctly?

"I also wondered if rebellion was the right course of action. I've talked to Arty about my thoughts, my anxieties and my fears. I told him I was really upset about the school's money. And, yes, I'm disgusted at what Mannering and his teachers are doing and how they're treating us. But he is still our Headmaster."

At that, even the Second and Third Form boys started to grumble.

"However, Arty and I always seem to think the same way. Now it's no different."

Soppy glanced at the boys with a wry smile.

"I listened. I pondered. Then I thought – no, I'm not putting up with this, either!"

The audience was amazed. What did she say?

"So, Charlotte... *No!* I'm not allowing that old git, Godfrey, to get away with this!"

The boys' jaws dropped.

"There's simply no alternative," Soppy concluded.

She turned once again to the crowd.

"So, let's teach them a lesson! Let's get stuck in! *Let's rebel!*"

Remarkably and quite unexpectedly a massive cheer erupted. So loud this time that it did blow the windows right out! Flakes of paint and splinters of wood from window-frames sprayed onto the ground below.

Chanting broke out, too.

"Soppy! Soppy! Soppy!" shouted joyous boys from all three Forms.

"Star! Star! Star!" yelled the girls.

* * *

Sebastian Bannister was sitting in the PE storeroom nearby having a quiet smoke. He almost swallowed his cigar when the sound came blasting its way through the room. He coughed and spluttered, spitting out the soggy brown remnants onto the floor. He looked around, trying to see what had caused this horrendous noise, got up to investigate and started to wander around outside the storeroom...

* * *

Back inside the Pavilion, Arty stood up again and cleared his throat. He spoke quietly and seriously as he addressed his audience for the last time.

"Let a vote decide this matter. Hands up all those in favour of a revolution."

Immediately – a forest of raised arms. Arty started to count, as did Brains, Sid and Soppy. Brains was the first to calculate that – of a possible one hundred and eighty pupils – every single one had voted 'yes'.

"By a unanimous decision, it has been settled." Arty flung his arms out to his side. Like a footballer who'd just scored a goal, he puffed out his chest, hung his head back and shouted out to the crowd...

"West Mayling is officially under revolt!"

Chapter 6

Operation Tixylix

Another cheer, the loudest of the afternoon, erupted in the Pavilion. The wave of sound vibrated through the inner rooms, shook the shower cubicles, then burst through the doors on to the arena outside. It blasted Bannister full in the face, knocking him back down the concrete steps, dropping him firmly onto his bottom on the grass below. Sebastian sat up, dazed and confused, his hair ruffled and his eyes crossed. The noise of eleven bells rang loudly in each ear.

* * *

Whilst this was happening outside, Arty called for quiet inside. He started to explain the plans that were about to be set in motion.

"We are going to call it 'Operation Tixylix.' Why? Well, we're going to take over the entire school, capture all the teachers... and give them a taste of their own medicine!"

An excited ripple of giggles followed.

"The takeover has to be co-ordinated, timely and

thorough. Above all, though, Operation Tixylix must be successful in every part. We've divided you up into smaller groups with a couple of Third Formers as your leaders. They've got instructions about which area you're to attack and which members of the staff you're to capture. If everything goes according to plan, the final showdown with God will be in the Staffroom at precisely four o'clock this afternoon. So, if there are no further questions... let the Revolution begin!"

Little did anyone know that Saturday afternoon would go down in history as one of West Mayling's most remarkable. The rebellion plans were excellent. Brains devised most of the key manoeuvres, with the others chipping in thoughts here and there. Brains pieced these together into the final jigsaw puzzle.

A contented smile adorned the faces of Arty and Brains as they saw Operation Tixylix taking shape. They looked on in admiration as each group listened intently to their instructions, completely focussed on the tasks in hand. The rebellion was well under way!

* * *

First to be taken care of was Sebastian Bannister. The pupils knew he went for a quiet smoke after every Saturday morning Sports Practice. The plan was to entrap him inside the storeroom, using the nets which normally held a variety of sports balls. A platoon of students would hurl empty nets onto Bannister, like an angler catching fish, then escort him off to the Staffroom.

However, since Sebastian Bannister had already been knocked for six by the enormous sound wave that exploded from the meeting, this plan was no longer needed. Big Tony found him still squatting on the grass at the bottom of the steps and realised that a much simpler plan would do. Walking across the top step, then slowly descending the rest of them, Tony started to untie his rugby boots.

Sebastian Bannister began to shake the cobwebs from his head and his vision began to regain focus. He saw Big Tony untying his laces and heard the rumble of noise in the background. Bannister's eyebrows furrowed and a look of annoyance cast over his face.

"Lincetti, what the hell's going on in there?"

Big Tony looked up at Bannister but stayed silent, ignoring his harsh and abrupt tone. He continued to unlace his boots.

"Didn't you hear me, Lincetti?" demanded the PE Teacher, fuming at the lack of response. "I asked you what was going on in there! Give me an answer, boy!"

Big Tony moved forward, one boot in his hand, the other still on his foot. He hobbled towards Bannister, still saying nothing.

"Lincetti, you ignorant oaf!" screeched Bannister. "You'll get two hours detention for this insolence! Do you hear me? Two hours!"

"Shut it, Bannister, you ignoramus!"

"What did you call me?" yelled Bannister, almost at boiling point, his face a dark crimson and his teeth gritted.

"You're all mouth, mouth, mouth!" retorted Big Tony. "You shout on the playing fields. You shout in the classroom. You shout in the corridor. Even when you're talking to someone face to face, you shout. What a prize berk!"

"Berk? *Berk?*" yelled Bannister. "Ahhh!"

Bannister jumped to his feet but he had to steady himself. The sudden movement had made him light-headed. Big Tony didn't panic. He was wiping his hand across the underneath of his boot. He scooped a large, sloppy mound of mud into a heap in his palm. Big Tony looked at the mud. Bannister looked at Big Tony. They both looked at each other. Big Tony smiled.

"Don't even think about it..." started Bannister, pointing his finger at Tony.

Tony kept smiling. He flicked his wrist at Bannister. The mound of mud slid off his palm and wobbled through the air. It was a good shot. It caught Bannister full in the face, splattering over his eyes, up his nostrils and into his mouth, shutting him up before he could utter any more threats. Bannister coughed and spluttered as he tripped backwards, once again landing on his bottom.

As Bannister spat out some grassy mud and removed parts of it from his face, Big Tony whistled to his platoon who had just appeared in the Pavilion doorway. They were looking on in wonder and disbelief, watching Sebastian receiving this surprise lunchtime 'snack'. They ran forward and grabbed Bannister by the arms. Assisted by Tony, they dragged him inside. Big Tony stepped behind Bannister, pulled out the tail of his shirt and grabbed the waist of his underpants.

Bannister let out a high-pitched yelp.

"What the hell are you playing at, Lincetti?"

Still ignoring him, Big Tony yanked Bannister upwards and hooked the elastic lining at the top of his pants onto one of the clothes pegs on the wall. Bannister sagged under his own body weight, while his pants stretched up the full length of his back. He remained suspended, kicking and screaming, with absolutely nowhere to go. He had been caught in what is more commonly known as a 'Wedgie'.

If you've never had the 'pleasure' of being put in a Wedgie, let me explain to you how it works. Nowadays, pants are built big and strong, and modern forms of elastic are tough enough to hold your full body weight. A Wedgie is quite literally having your underpants grabbed from behind, yanked firmly upwards and then, generally, hung on a hook. The pressure on the posterior, as you might imagine, can be painful. It is also embarrassing and humiliating to be hung, completely defenceless, on a peg. All you can do is move like a puppet on a string – like one of those in 'Thunderbirds'. Everyone looks on and laughs at your misfortune.

So that's what a Wedgie is – very unpleasant and something you never forget. If you learn nothing else from this book, remember this – avoid a Wedgie like you'd avoid the plague!

Everybody doubled up with laughter and cheered at Bannister's situation. His face turned gradually from anger to a sheepish, defeated look of surrender. He stopped kicking and shouting. Arty walked forward, stood next to Bannister and crossed his arms.

"Welcome to you, Mr Bannister! Welcome!" he said, smiling.

"Fox, what on earth is going on?" demanded Bannister. "This is an outrage, do you hear? An outrage! Of all the pupils here at West Mayling, I would never have put you, Arthur Fox, in the midst of any of it!"

"Pipe down, Sebastian!" Arty replied casually, causing the others to chuckle at his contemptuous tone. "It's not your turn to talk, it's ours. I just wanted to welcome you as our first... ummm... 'guest'... at the official opening of West Mayling's Rebellion!"

"Rebellion?" gasped Bannister. "You'll never get away with it! The Headmaster will have you all branded and expelled for this! He'll publicly denounce you and ruin the rest of your school lives! You'll never get into another decent school again! Do you understand me, Fox? You'll all suffer for this! You're finished. You're through! You're toast!"

"Typical PE Teacher!" tutted Arty. "Loves the sound of his own voice! Well, if you love PE that much, Sebastian, we will have to give you something you can really get your teeth into, shan't we?"

* * *

The next few minutes were indeed a spectacular sight! Bannister was taken down from his 'perch' and escorted through the mud towards the middle of the rugby field. There, he was tied to the front of the scrum machine with several skipping ropes, whilst some of the First Formers leapt on the back of it.

In case you weren't aware, a scrum machine is what rugby players use to practise a part of their game. A scrum is when eight men link together and push against another eight men who are pushing back in the opposite direction. To practise this, a machine that looks like a large, three-sided, Roman chariot is used, against which one lot of eight men can push. The machine has a front and two sides, but no back to it. It rests on wheels so it can move over the field surface when it is pushed. At the front of the scrum machine are padded shoulder rests, against which the front three rugby players push. Other men stand in the trolley to add weight to the machine.

It was to these shoulder rests that Sebastian Bannister was tied. The only slight difference was that, instead of facing towards the scrum machine, he was facing away from it. This now resembled a horse and cart. And it was exactly like a horse pulling a cart that Bannister was encouraged to act, pulling the First Formers around the soggy pitch time and time again.

Bannister puffed and panted as he struggled with the weight of the scrum machine and its occupants, but he did manage to 'wheeze' his way around six times. The rest of the pupils watched, applauding him vigorously. As he fell to his knees, completely exhausted and drained of energy, Big Tony and Mitch McGovern picked him up and dragged him towards the main school buildings.

"Didn't young Sebastian enjoy his lovely PE lesson today?" enquired Mitch sarcastically. "No? Well, now you're finding out how we feel every time we have one of yours!"

* * *

So that was Sebastian Bannister taken care of. But he was only one teacher. His capture was always going to be easy because he was stuck out in the playing fields, miles from the main school buildings. Arty knew that capturing the other teachers – without attracting the attention of their colleagues – would be a much harder job. However, Brains said he had taken this into consideration and he was sure that his plans would work...

Chapter 7

Ooh La La!

"Mais, oui!" had been Soppy's reply, when she was asked to take charge of this operation. Her objective was the capture of Philippe Saint-Moreaux, the French Teacher.

Soppy led her group up to the Staff Quarters on the first floor. As they approached The Saint's room, though, they heard *two* voices. Soppy listened carefully and realised that the other PE Teacher, Barbara Alison, was also with Philippe Saint-Moreaux.

"Two for the price of one," thought Soppy. "That's fine by me!"

She turned to look at Charlotte O'Driscoll. Charlotte looked back with a bashful smile and pointed towards the door.

"Is that... Barbara Alison in there... with The Saint?" she enquired.

"Oh, yes!" replied Soppy, smiling.

"The saucy old git!" whispered Charlotte, slapping her hand over her mouth, embarrassed at what they'd discovered. "I don't believe it! I wouldn't have thought she was his type. I'd have thought he'd have gone for a scholar or a linguist or someone like that."

"Maybe he fancied something a little more 'sporty', Charlie!" suggested Soppy, making both of them giggle hysterically. Now the rest of the girls started giggling too, though trying hard not to make too much noise. Soppy hushed them up, still smiling, but remembering that she had a job to do – a task of great importance.

She crept closer to the door and peered through the keyhole. She saw Saint-Moreaux and Barbara Alison sitting in armchairs. He was reading the newspaper, she was sipping a cup of tea. Soppy didn't think anything of this. What she *did* think strange was that they were both sitting there in only their underwear!

"Ooh la la!" she said.

Soppy blinked. She had to look twice to help it sink in. She shook her head. It was all a bit sad rather than romantic. After all, it wasn't a pretty sight!

The Saint was in his fifties. He still carried a good head of longish brown hair. But he did look a bit ancient. Deep wrinkles wound round his eyes and his skin was grey and weathered.

Barbara Alison – just in her thirties – was definitely too thin for comfort. Her ribs could be seen through her paper-thin skin and her limbs were quite puny as well. Soppy shook her head again. Barbara needed a good square meal, she thought. In fact three or four Sunday roasts wouldn't go amiss. Whatever food was necessary, though, Soppy believed she ought to give up that disgusting smoking habit. It was probably this that gave her the appearance of a broomstick.

The group split up into two halves, one staying outside the door, the other creeping round onto the balcony at the back of the room. Soppy swallowed hard... then knocked on the door. The Saint put his bathrobe on and answered it. As soon as the door was opened, Soppy gave the order and the girls burst through at speed. Immediately, a Second Former, Jasmine Archer, raced to the window. She unhooked the safety latch so the others outside could enter.

Soppy looked quickly around the room. Ignoring The Saint's outburst of profanities, she noticed he'd left a pair of braces on the back of an armchair. She grabbed them quickly and nodded to the other girls. Charlotte O'Driscoll swooped down from behind The Saint and jumped onto his back, wrapping her arms around his neck and covering up his eyes. Amidst yet more unrepeatable cursing from The Saint, Charlotte held on for dear life as two other First Formers, Jayne Briars and Hortence Flowers, grabbed his arms and stopped him from wriggling. Moving rapidly, Soppy tied the braces around his wrists. She then grabbed his silk tie and wound it round his ankles, completely locking his appendages together.

Whilst this was happening, Barbara Alison looked on, static from shock. Jasmine watched her intensely. When she thought the PE Teacher was about to help out, Jasmine jumped into action. Grabbing a china cup filled with tea and a matching china bowl full of sugar, she threw the contents of both over the teacher. Barbara Alison let out a screech of horror as she turned from an undressed PE Teacher into a sweet-smelling, tea-stained, shrieking wreck. Showing no mercy whatsoever, Jasmine took Barbara Alison's silk scarf and ripped it down the middle, creating two thinner strips. She tied one around the sobbing teacher's wrists and the other around her sticky, sugar-coated ankles.

Job done! Two more teachers totally trussed, ready for delivery to the Staffroom. Soppy called for Arty to join them and he duly arrived a few minutes later. He ticked off their names from his list and glanced over at the undressed members of staff.

"How embarrassing!" he said out aloud, causing both teachers to blush. "But it gives me a good idea."

* * *

The overall plan was to capture the teachers who were located on the outskirts of the buildings first, then slowly move inwards towards the Staffroom. Here, everyone was eventually going to be held. Sebastian Bannister, Philippe Saint-Moreaux and Barbara Alison had already been caught. They were secured in a cupboard in the Staffroom, guarded by some Second Form boys.

Now it was Cook's turn, as the Kitchen was also one of the most distant rooms. The Cook would be there for certain, conjuring up yet another dire attempt at 'nouveau-cuisine' to be served that evening for dinner. Agnes Brewer was well known for her 'Cajun' cooking. Actually, she only used the term Cajun to mask the fact that she always burnt everything, from toast to gravy and from custard to pork chops and porridge. Everything was black, crusty, and tasting as though it had been left on a barbecue all summer.

It was the task of Sid and his fellow saboteurs to capture the Cook and escort her to the Staffroom, too.

* * *

The group were surprised to find a delicious, sweet odour wafting its way along the corridor that led to the Kitchens. It was the smell of freshly-baked cookies – nice tasty ones at that! Sid and his team were caught completely off guard by this unique event.

"Don't tell me that, just at the very point we're about to seize old Agnes, she actually manages to cook something edible!" he remarked.

Well, of course, their new hopes about old Agnes were turned on their head. Bursting through the Kitchen door, they saw dozens of recently emptied paper bags scattered around on the surface. Each bag carried the logo of West Mayling's local bakery. Alongside, fragrant, freshly-made cookies had been heaped onto decorated plates for the next Staff Meeting – but *not* freshly-baked by Agnes!

"Told you it was too good to be true," chuckled Blankets.

Capturing Agnes Brewer was no mean feat. She may have been sixty-six years old, but they were soon to find out that she was tough as old nails and gave new meaning to the phrase 'old battle-axe'. Grey-haired, with a calm Scottish accent, she was well-liked by the children even though she couldn't cook for toffee.

Agnes Brewer's Kitchen was totally her own territory which was strictly out of bounds. So, when Sid's group burst into her space, this mild-mannered Cook turned suddenly into an adrenalin-charged, hyperactive grizzly bear. One that had just been stung by a wasp. Grabbing a silver saucepan in her left hand and a char-grill frying pan in her right, the now demented old chef proceeded to swipe at anything that came within swinging distance of her or her cookies.

'No go' to old Agnes meant 'no go'!

Sid and the others ducked and dived, furiously trying to avoid being walloped into oblivion. They began to doubt whether this rebellion was quite such a good idea!

It was Blankets McDougal who came up with the life-saving action. He jumped up onto a work surface to escape her swipes. As he moved, he knocked over a few of Cook's tins. These contained her own home-made cookies and cakes. He guessed they'd taste worse than a mouldy frog left to dry out under a scorching sun. This gave him an idea. He grabbed a handful of mashed cookies and took aim in Agnes' direction.

"Cook!" he yelled. "Look out!"

As Agnes turned to face Blankets, Sid stamped hard on her foot. Agnes opened her mouth to howl just as the handful of cookies left Blankets. Instead of shouting, as planned, Agnes found several chunks of cookie entering her mouth. Swallowing these – for the first time in her life – made Agnes turn a subtle green colour. She pirouetted around and soon passed out from the excruciatingly vile taste!

"So much for that sweet, old, Granny figure they call the Cook," said Sid. "What a maniac!"

"Maybe," joked Blankets, "but, like Arty said, this is Operation Tixylix and she certainly got a taste of her own medicine!"

Sid sent a First Former to collect Arty. Arty crossed Cook off his list and started chatting to Sid. Hearing the full story of how they – or rather her cookies – had eventually overpowered old Agnes, Arty began to ponder again.

"You know, eating cookies gives me another good idea." But he didn't explain what he had in mind...

* * *

Capturing the rest of the staff wasn't likely to be the forced physical affair that it had been so far. Brains had stated that they would be much easier to catch if they could be brought together in one group.

A letter was slipped under the door of the six remaining teachers and Devinia, saying:

> 'Staff Party in the Staffroom at four.
> Have your slice of cake – and eat it!'

Brains knew this could be a flaw in their plans. If any of the staff didn't believe that the letter was genuine, they might not come to the meeting. That would make it impossible for the pupils to capture them all together. It might even undermine the entire rebellion. Brains, however, took this calculated risk. He guessed they'd be too greedy to resist. The one exception would be Pablo. The introverted Art Teacher wouldn't want to party with his colleagues. That didn't matter, anyway. Although most of the teachers did find it baffling, luckily for Brains it worked.

The staff thought these words were a cryptic clue, perhaps meaning the Head was going to discuss their Retirement Fund? They chuckled to themselves, rubbed their hands in glee and waited for four o'clock to arrive...

* * *

At the appointed time, five teachers – no Durrant – and Devinia made their way to the Staffroom. The pupils, meanwhile, had hidden themselves at various points en route ready for the ensuing battle.

Arriving at the Staffroom, the teachers were surprised to be greeted by Arty Fox. He was sitting alone in an armchair in the centre of the room. His legs were crossed, while he calmly sipped a glass of what looked like the Headmaster's brandy. It was, in fact, a glass of cold tea, no milk, one sugar!

The staff halted in their tracks. They stood aghast at this pupil taking such a liberty, the likes of which had never been seen at West Mayling House. Dusty Clive Shaw, the Latin Teacher, stepped forward and looked in disgust at Arty.

"Fox!" he exclaimed. "Get out of here! And put that brandy back, you thief!"

"Nuts!" Arty snapped back.

"What?"

"I said 'nuts', you overpaid, highly-strung imbecile!"

"What? How dare you, Fox!"

"Nuts, again!" repeated Arty indignantly.

"Have you totally lost your mind, Fox?" shouted Dr Reynolds, the Maths Teacher.

"You can stick your long division up your diameter, Reynolds!" retorted Arty. Brains and Soppy, who were hiding behind one of the chairs, cringed in disbelief. "This is a rebellion, you know, and you're all under our control now. So nuts to you!"

"A rebellion?" chuckled Dusty Shaw, looking round the room. "What rebellion, you idiot! Where? How? All by yourself? What are you, drunk or something? What sort of rebellion is it, when only *one* young fool rebels?"

Arty whistled.

The other students in the room, who had been hiding behind furniture, too, stood up. The staff looked startled. All around them were children armed with handfuls of cookies and cakes and containers full of a heavy, gooey mixture of dough!

Dickie Howard, the English Teacher, was standing at the back of the group. He turned and stepped out of the doorway. He glanced up the stairs, only to see a barricade of upturned desks and chairs right across the top of the Landing. Behind this defensive line was Fatty Balshaw, backed by a number of Second Formers, each armed with catapults.

Dickie Howard looked down the corridor towards the Kitchen exit. He saw in horror that this had been blocked off by four settees grouped neatly together, two on top of two. These formed another unbreakable barrier. Behind this stood Charlotte O'Driscoll, Sid, Blankets McDougal and a few others holding buckets full of disgusting cold gravy or used washing-up water.

The English Teacher moved his line of sight towards the Front Door. The massive door opened slowly to reveal Mitch McGovern who was standing there holding a rugby ball. Known as the supreme school athlete, Mitch was strong and muscular – and highly competitive. Today, he looked particularly cross and miserable, with a 'don't even think about it' look on his face. Dickie Howard simply turned round and gulped.

"Surrounded are you, Dickie?" asked Arty smugly.

The other staff turned to face Dickie Howard for an explanation of Arty's words.

"Yes... we're completely surrounded," whispered Howard, rather worried that what Arty was claiming might be turning into reality.

"What?" shouted Dr Reynolds. "Surrounded? What on earth do you mean, surrounded?"

"Goodness me!" shouted Arty. "Are you thick or something, Rupert? When Dickie says 'surrounded' he means... 'surrounded'. You know, something like a circumference, a complete circle around you. I'd have thought a great mathematician like you would have understood such a simple concept. Dear, oh dear, what a fraud!"

Reynolds' face looked a picture of embarrassment. As his colour changed to bright pink, the rest of the pupils burst out laughing. Arty stood up and walked forward.

"Right! You now know that this is a *serious* rebellion. You now know that all exits are secured and that you're surrounded. You know that you can't escape. What you don't know is what's going to happen next. Well, it's simple... we're going to get the Head in here. We're going to talk through a few

93

things. Then, we're going to call the police. Unless, of course, we can come to an alternative solution..."

Brains now walked forward and cleared his throat. He faced Devinia Longchamps, the Headmaster's personal Secretary.

"As you are Godfrey's closest colleague here, Miss Longchamps, we have decided that it will be you who goes and fetches the Head."

"Me?" whimpered Devinia Longchamps.

"Yes, you, Devinia," snapped Arty. "So belt up and get cracking!"

"I say!" interrupted Wellington Waters, the History Teacher. "Steady on, young Fox! You should respect your elders, you know!"

"Nuts!" was Arty's response.

Chapter 8

'Veni, Vidi, Vici'

This brings us back to the point where you joined us at the beginning of this book. Devinia Longchamps had wobbled along the corridor, been hit by a soft gooey lump hurtling from Fatty's catapult, and raced through her room into Godfrey Mannering's Office. She'd then blurted out about the whole revolution saga. Leaving Devinia cowering in his Office, the Headmaster stormed down the corridor, into the Staffroom and confronted this pesky little 'headache' called Arty Fox. Then the stand-off ensued.

* * *

It would be quite hard to imagine exactly what the Headmaster and his band of teachers were feeling at this point. They assumed they were soon to retire, each with a great pot of gold. They thought they enjoyed complete control of the school. Then, suddenly, a barrage of heavily-armed, cheeky, young brats comes roving into view, demanding that they all bow down and admit to their sins.

Well, Godfrey Randolph Mannering obviously wasn't having any of that. Pointing at the students, he glared at the terrified teachers and bellowed out his commands.

"Get in there, you bunch of wet tissues! Sort them out. Now!"

* * *

Nobody ever thought God could lose his temper. He was always so serene, so composed. He'd never been known to rant or rave. No-one had ever seen him 'lose it'.

Not like this.

Even the teachers were afraid of him now. Both fear and the urge to fulfil their greedy desires spurred the staff on. They obeyed God's commands without question. They charged hell-for-leather in a forward assault.

Brains had warned Arty that a counter-attack could be possible, so they *must* be prepared in advance. Little did the staff know just how prepared the pupils could be...

* * *

First casualty was Agnes Brewer.

Agnes switched once again from sweet and innocent to vicious and warrior-like. She rolled up her sleeves and charged towards Arty. He stepped aside smartly, leaving the way clear for Brains to take aim with a portion of dough. Agnes stopped dead as she ducked to avoid it. A good job she did because it went straight through the wooden wall panels and fractured the brickwork beyond! Wow! Brains looked at Arty, Arty at Brains. No wonder Cook's dough made such perfect rock cakes!

Agnes, of course, was still on the loose...

Soppy stepped in as second line of defence. She'd planned to bombard the staff with Cook's vile, indigestible cookies. She scooped up a bowl-full of the pre-crumbled mix and hurled it high above Agnes. Cook copped a mouthful from the downpour of semi-poisonous mush. She coughed and spluttered, attempting to spit it out. Too late! She rapidly turned once again to a subtle shade of dark green, belched deeply and passed out. She fell in a heap on the floor.

* * *

Next were Sebastian Bannister and Dr Rupert Reynolds. These two made a terribly miscalculated error. They tried to escape past Mitch McGovern.

Mitch was not in the mood to be messed with, especially by these particular teachers. Although he didn't mind Maths, Reynolds' wretched homeworks drove Mitch mad. He actually loved sports, but could never forgive Bannister for the false accusations that had so hurt his pride. Adding these thoughts together, Mitch arrived at an answer of 'Four'.

Four?

"Yes," Mitch decided, "*four* lovely black eyes! The number I intend to dish out!"

He looked down at the array of missiles spread out on the floor in front of him. He ran his fingers over his lips, debating which object to send first. The old-fashioned, leather-cased rugby ball looked odds-on favourite to start with. This was mainly because of its very hard exterior and the way it stung your hands if you tried to catch it. He picked it up and – poised like a javelin thrower – propelled it directly at Bannister. Unfortunately the ball spun too fast and veered just off course.

"Missed, you useless oaf!" shouted the PE Teacher.

However, Sebastian hadn't been paying attention to where he was running. Whilst watching the ball zoom past him, he ran head first into the school bell which hung on a strong, steel bracket attached to the wall. Catching this great brass bell full on, Bannister let out a rasping "Owww!" and held his nose with both hands. The bell usually sounded the end of one lesson and the start of the next. This time it signalled the end for Sebastian and the start of the end for Reynolds.

Mitch bent down and picked up a handful of baseballs. "Yo, Rupert – catch!" he shouted, lobbing them gently at Reynolds. This took the Maths Teacher totally by surprise. He found himself jigging from side to side attempting to catch the balls. With his mind now completely off guard, he lurched into an already stunned Sebastian Bannister. Sebastian, presuming he was under renewed attack, instinctively lashed out, thumping his oppressor, Reynolds, on his nose too. Bashed, bruised and thoroughly beaten, they both came to rest alongside the Front Door under the bemused gaze of Mitch.

Mitch just stood, with hands on hips, watching the fiasco unfold.

He leant over the dishevelled heap.

"Hmmm. Let me see," he started. "One black eye... Add one... Add another... Add one more... equals... four! Ah-ha! You see, Doc. Despite your lousy teaching, I've managed to learn some Maths after all. Mitch McGovern, brains as well as brawn. Don't you agree, *Sebastian?*"

* * *

Meanwhile, Wellington Waters, Barbara Alison, Philippe Saint-Moreaux, Dusty Clive Shaw and Dickie Howard had made for the Kitchen area which had been blocked off by the four large settees. They were the old type of sofa, with solid wooden frame, massive padding and robust, traditional springs. Behind them stood Charlotte O'Driscoll, Blankets McDougal and Sid, holding buckets of beautiful goo.

The teachers hadn't spotted the assortment of

goods that were lined up, ready and waiting, so they blundered blindly towards the settees. They grimaced and growled, trying hard to scare the pupils into a hasty retreat. The children stood firm and took aim.

First to chuck was Sid. He closed his left eye and homed in on Shaw. With a carefully calculated swing of his arms, Sid sent a tidal wave of the most foul-smelling, mouldiest gravy ever witnessed at West Mayling House. Shaw was completely engulfed. It felt like being slapped on the cheeks by a shoal of wet kippers. With his eyelids sealed by the thick, greasy slime, he lost all sense of direction. He trod on Mitch's rugby ball, which had landed nearby, and spiralled down the side of the corridor. He collided abruptly with the School Trophy Cabinet, which brought him to rest with a bang!

Charlotte was next to react. As Barbara Alison advanced, she hurled a bucket of filthy dish-water full of left-over scraps from their plates. She had nothing against Alison personally, but believed she had bad taste in men generally and Philippe Saint-Moreaux in particular. Charlotte thought he was a creepy old 'charmer', fit for nothing but a hefty kick where it hurt. What a delight for Charlotte, therefore, when her contents missed Barbara – who'd ducked – but met The Saint full on!

"Vive La France!" she shouted, clapping her hands with glee.

The deluge completely smothered The Saint.

Soggy lumps brushed past his taste buds, sending warning signals up to his brain. He shuddered and shivered, and his muscles seized up. Frozen like a statue, he skated across the greasy surface, somersaulted over Dusty Shaw and whacked the cabinet with his feet. The cabinet shook and the brackets gave way. It crashed to the floor with a resounding thud, scattering trophies and plates far and wide.

By ducking so low to avoid Charlotte's bucket-load, Barbara Alison had lost her balance. She now tripped clumsily over her own naked feet but her momentum shot her forward into the barricade. She collapsed into the cushioned padding at the base of a settee but the powerful springs recoiled, rocketing her back swiftly from whence she came. Sprinting backwards over the slippery floor, Alison skidded into both Dickie Howard and Wellington Waters, who were only a few steps behind. Alison's skinny elbows caught Dickie and Wellie neatly between their ribs. Entwined and winded, all three teachers toppled over backwards on to the Inter-School Cross-Country Championship Plate, smashing it into a mosaic of more than a thousand colourful pieces.

* * *

Leaving the teachers groaning on the corridor floor, Charlotte O'Driscoll went to fetch Paul Pablo

Durrant, the Art Teacher, from his living quarters.

As Brains had surmised, Paul Pablo Durrant had not understood his cryptic letter. He'd *certainly* not wanted to join in with a 'jelly and ice cream' party with the other 'non-creative' teachers. He'd therefore remained inside his quarters. While listening to Bach and painting some fruit, he missed all the fun and games taking place on the floor below him.

Arriving outside his room, Charlotte knocked on the door firmly, then waited. It opened slowly.

"Sir, you're required in the Staffroom. Arty Fox wishes you to join your colleagues there."

"Really?"

"Yes... You see, there seems to have been a bit of a rebellion."

"Really?"

"Yes. It looks like the teachers have been captured and taken prisoner."

"Oh!"

"Yes," continued Charlotte, amazed by Durrant's vagueness and lack of concern. "So, being the victors, we need you downstairs... like... straight away."

"Righty-ho!" chirped Durrant blankly. "I will come down when I've got my charcoals and sketchpad!"

Charlotte looked on in amazement. She shook her head. "Whatever."

* * *

That just left the Headmaster, Godfrey Randolph Mannering, who had been the instigator of this disgraceful, riotous outburst by the teachers. He now became the main target – and he certainly got his fair share of pelting!

Fatty Balshaw was positioned on the first floor Landing, overlooking the chaotic scenes below. He saw Godfrey charge out of the Staffroom and was determined to stop him. His catapult was armed and ready with a mouldy plum. He let rip as soon as Godfrey set foot into the corridor. The plum was targeted at the Head's forehead and it met its objective with a resounding 'splat' – the smelly inner juices scattering evenly over Godfrey's face.

Godfrey immediately retreated into the Staffroom where Soppy stood armed with another bowl of mix to fling over him. Mannering tried to shield himself by wrapping his arms around his face. No chance! A few morsels entered his mouth and started to dissolve on his tongue. The Head tried hard to resist regurgitating this cocktail of unspeakable ingredients from the Cook. With eyes bulging and cheeks pouting he soon failed. A stream of gooey vomit hurtled between his teeth and splashed over the School Prospectus which lay neatly on the staff's coffee table!

Godfrey Mannering wiped his mouth and cursed. "Little beggars," he muttered under his breath. He shook his head, then staggered forward into the doorway between the Staffroom and the corridor.

Dazed, he stood wondering which way to go. Bodies to the left... Bodies to the right... Straight ahead, then?

Fatty Balshaw, meanwhile, had ordered his Second Form group to reload their catapults with more fruit. When Godfrey appeared they took aim... and fired! A rainbow of fruit hailed down on the Head. Each piece exploded on impact, creating a spectrum of mush over his gown.

"Look!" shouted Fatty. "It's Godfrey and his Amazing Multicoloured Fruit-coat!"

Mannering stood up straight. Looking particularly annoyed by Fatty's comment, he took a deep breath, then attempted to storm up the stairs. Another barrage of fruit came his way, squelching into the target from all angles.

This bombardment slowed Godfrey down to one step at a time. But he persevered – one arm clutching the bannister, the other covering his face. The fruit rained down relentlessly, more mushy by the second.

Still Godfrey ascended, seemingly unstoppable, whilst the crate began to look extremely sparse...

Doubts entered Fatty's mind. Could they hold the Head off for much longer? All that Fatty now had left – right at the bottom of his crate – were two halves of ageing watermelon. He reached down and picked up the first. He rested it in his palm under his chin. Holding his other arm out straight, like a shot-put thrower, he launched the melon at the approaching Head.

The melon soared gracefully through the air,

catching Godfrey full in the face. The inner pulp sloshed out, leaving the green outer skin covering all his facial features. Godfrey Mannering had, finally, been stopped in his tracks.

"Your moisturising face-mask, Sir!" smiled Fatty.

The melon skin slid slowly off Godfrey's face. Once again, Fatty assumed the shot-put position and lobbed the second piece. This followed the same perfect trajectory as the first, splatting all over the Head's frowning face.

"And there's your deep-cleanse and tone!"

This time the impact knocked Godfrey off balance. Much to the relief of the children on the Landing, they saw him tumble backwards, head-over-heels down the stairs. The children stopped and stared. A sticky bundle of Headmaster wrapped in his gown arrived on the ground floor. Godfrey lay flat on his back, his body motionless.

The Entrance Hall fell silent.

The Grandfather Clock ticked.

Nothing stirred.

Devinia popped her head out of her Office for a second, witnessed the carnage – then hastily retreated to safety.

Suddenly, like a Cyborg, Godfrey's head rose an inch. One eye opened. The children drew a sharp breath.

Godfrey scanned the ceiling and the surrounding walls. No-one dared move a muscle.

But Godfrey could feel his body aching from head to toe. He let out a deflated sigh and his head dropped back to the floor.

Defeat.

Jubilant cheers and uproar!

The storm had passed.

* * *

The students stopped and surveyed the scene. Most of the teachers were lying stranded on the floor, mown down by one method or another. Cuthbertson had long ago passed out behind the settee – defunct, but emitting an occasional belch. Their guiding light and leader, Godfrey Randolph Mannering, the Head, lay bedraggled at the bottom of the staircase.

Pablo sat stunned at the top of the stairs...

Arty and Brains emerged from the Staffroom and confronted the bewildered, beleaguered, defeated Headmaster.

"Do you yield, Godfrey?" asked Arty.

"What? Er? Who? Er? *You!* Nuts!" replied the Head.

Arty stepped forward and looked round at his fellow pupils and friends. He placed his foot on top of the Head's chest, raised a clenched fist and held it next to his heart.

"'Veni, Vidi, Vici' as the great Julius Caesar once said, 'I came, I saw, I conquered'!"

Pay-back

Chapter 9

Showing Too Much Cheek!

A celebratory meal was in order. After all, the students had earned it. Success had to be rewarded. Pay-back had to start somewhere.

Well, it all happened that night. The meal was booked for seven o'clock sharp in the Dining Hall. This time, wearing school uniform was definitely not compulsory. Nor was the time available to eat your meal limited to fifteen minutes. Another 'first' – there was going to be choice on the menu. And what's more you could eat your courses in whatever order you desired!

The intention was to have a jolly fine feast, with all food and beverages kindly donated by Godfrey Randolph Mannering from his private store in the school cellars. However, when the Four Musketeers entered the basement expecting to see a massive collection of boxes, crates, cans and bottles, that was not quite what they found...

"Are you sure this is where he keeps all the *good* stuff?" asked Arty.

"Positive," said Brains.

"Well, I hate to disappoint you... but I can't see a hoard of goodies down here."

"Nonsense! You're not looking in the right place. This is Godfrey's personal collection of..." Brains entered the vast expanse of empty space. "I don't believe it! There should be wall-to-wall crates and boxes down here, enough to make a restaurant jealous."

"Arty, what's the matter?" called Soppy from the staircase behind them.

"It's old Godfrey."

"What about him?"

"Well, I'd say he's a bloomin' cheapskate, Sops!"

"Why? What's wrong?"

"Not a sausage..." huffed Brains, sifting through a few of the broken boxes. "Oh... well, a couple of vegetarian ones, perhaps."

"Sops, it looks like Brains' idea for a 'Gourmet Feast', packed with the finest meats, pastries, cakes and chocolates is going to be short of just one thing –"

"What's that?"

"Er... the finest meats, pastries, chocolates and cakes, I guess!"

"Well, there goes our celebratory meal then," groaned Sid.

"Not necessarily, Sid. The meal can still go ahead. Not quite in the style we had planned, but with the best goodies we can find in Agnes' Kitchen. Brains, is there anything at all that we *can* use down there?"

"Yesss... yet another tin of rice pudding to add to our collection upstairs... there's some old dried prunes.. a mile or so of spaghetti... oh... from 1974... a box of mouldy apples... three cartons of cranberry juice... and a pack of Danish bacon."

"Mmmm," said Sid sarcastically, "that sounds tasty. Maybe we can blend them all together and have a giant fruit lasagne!"

"Brains, are there... er... any beverages down there, perchance?"

"Actually, yes, there are."

"Excellent! What's there?"

"Herbal tea!"

"Herbal tea?"

"Yep! Herbal tea."

"What – no bottles of 'Taittinger '88'? No brandy? No port?"

"It gets worse!" Sid tutted. "The tipple for the victors is... *herbal tea?* Oh, this simply isn't cricket, Arty!"

"You're right, Sid, it isn't cricket... it's a herbal drink!"

"So, what do you suggest now?" asked Soppy.

"I've got it!" snapped Arty. "I'll get some of Cook's home-made 'Medicinal Brew' and fill these empty bottles with it. We'll mix it with milk. That should spice it up a bit!"

"Oh, no!" swallowed Sid. "Not that terrible stuff she makes you drink when you're ill. It's horrible!"

"Too right!" added Soppy. "Medicinal Brew sends you light-headed and plays havoc with your bowels!"

"That's as maybe," continued Arty, "but it will keep everybody happy tonight. Besides, there's a huge supply of toilet paper down here, so where's the problem?"

It was agreed. Old Agnes Brewer's Medicinal Brew – made out of quite the most bizarre ingredients – was poured into the bottles. The Four Musketeers added semi-skimmed milk and a variety of flavoured custard powders. This produced a drink that was frothy, creamy and tasty as well as being a deep cleanser for your inner colon.

Soppy got together with Charlotte O'Driscoll to create a Fruit Punch. They decided it should consist of every fruit known to man, along with a pinch of herbal tea and a dash of Medicinal Brew for good measure.

However, a mass vomiting session was not on the planned list of events, so the experimental drinks were dished out according to age. First Formers were allowed to guzzle only milk, with the range on offer being skimmed, semi-skimmed or a hearty full cream indulgence. Second Formers were allowed to try Soppy and Charlotte's Fruit Punch as well. Only the Third Formers were allowed to delve into the spicy Medicinal Brew. This had been cunningly labelled 'Caribbean Cocktail'... but it still tasted awful.

A student bar of sorts, therefore, was ready for their feast.

* * *

Seven o'clock saw the massive flock of angels stampede into the Dining Hall more like a herd of wild elephants. Every table was crammed with excited students all yacking furiously amongst themselves, reflecting on their victory and looking forward to the evening's entertainment.

But at this point it is probably best to rewind the clocks once again...

* * *

Arty had just left his fruity shoe-print on the Head's chest following the final victory. He had insisted on the Head uttering – in public – the words "I yield". Godfrey and the teachers were then dragged into the Staffroom to meet with a few select members of the Third Form.

The arrangements the students had in mind were 'discussed'. First, the Head was forced to admit that plans were indeed afoot to embezzle the school's fee money. Godfrey only did so after three consecutive demands from Arty who had picked up the telephone and actually dialled through to the local Police.

The Head finally gave in.

Now Arty forced each of the adults to sign a declaration. It was cleverly worded. First, the staff had to admit their part in the embezzlement plot. Secondly, they had to agree not to try any further counter-attack. If such action did take place, the Police would be called immediately. That would certainly lead to the staff being prosecuted and probably suffering a lengthy spell in jail. An excellent deterrent!

Finally, the adults agreed to carry out all the 'reasonable' requests made by the children.

Reluctantly, they signed.

What an interesting development for the West Mayling Code of Silence!

* * *

Meanwhile, Arty had been chatting with his friends. They decided a celebratory meal was required that evening, with the teachers doing the cooking then serving as waiters and waitresses for the rest of the night. Godfrey's stock of gourmet foods and wines was to be consumed.

One of the students' requirements for the evening's entertainment was something that Arty had thought of after he had observed the capture of Philippe Saint-Moreaux and Barbara Alison earlier that afternoon. It may have sounded ludicrous, unnecessary perhaps. It certainly made the others giggle uncontrollably, but it *was* now going to happen...

So, what was this new demand? It was simple. Whilst cooking and serving that night, staff had to be dressed *only* in their underwear!

"This sounds *reasonable* enough to me!" Arty declared.

"You must be out of your mind, Fox!" exclaimed the Headmaster.

"If I remember rightly, *Godfrey*, your staff seem to spend half their weekends in *just* their underpants!"

"Damned cheek!" insisted Dr Reynolds.

"You lot won't get away with this!" added Dickie Howard.

"The subject is not open to negotiation, Muppet!" replied Arty. He picked up the phone and redialled the Police. The Head bit his lip and furrowed his eyebrows.

"Alright! Alright! You win!" he huffed. He shook his head and looked away from Arty. "But I warn you, Fox. I'll be back to get you!"

"Nuts!" said Arty.

* * *

The meal kicked off at seven sharp. Soppy and the six boys were seated at the Top Table. They stood up to encourage the rest of the students to quieten down. Soppy then said Grace.

Next, Brains addressed the crowd. He thanked everyone for their efforts, praising the younger First Formers especially for holding their nerve and seeing the job through to the end.

Arty followed by explaining the points to which the teachers had agreed earlier on in the Staffroom. The students were particularly relieved that the staff weren't going to try any further counter-attack. They knew this meant things wouldn't be so tense or fraught with danger. They felt they could now relax a little and enjoy the festivities to come!

Well, they were certainly going to enjoy those, only *far* more than anyone had expected...

The speeches ended. The vast array of food – tasty, though not as gourmet as hoped – was ready to be brought forth from the Kitchens. Then the first of that night's colossal uproars began.

Out walked the Head pushing a trolley laden with dessert. He was dressed simply in his shiny black shoes with matching black socks, Y-fronts in azure blue with a smart, white, sleeveless vest. The students collapsed in total hysterics, all clapping, laughing, whooping and cheering.

Funnier still was the traditional black mortarboard Godfrey Mannering still wore proudly poised upon his head. The contrast between this symbol of authority and the actual Headmaster – surrounded by pudding and standing in his pants – was unbelievably hilarious. Arty couldn't help but give way to a little wry grin. He turned to Brains and Sid to shake their hands and gave Soppy a big, brotherly hug. They had indeed won. They had accomplished something which just two nights ago was beyond their wildest dreams.

Following the Head were Barbara Alison and Philippe Saint-Moreaux, in the same underwear as when they were caught earlier on. Barbara Alison was close to tears from an embarrassment enhanced by the 'wolf-whistles' coming from the Second Form boys. Not to be outdone, though, the First and Second Form girls joined in. They cheered loudly for The Saint and threw crumpled up serviettes towards him. The Saint was as embarrassed as Barbara Alison. His tacky taste in boxer shorts was revealed – a large French flag embroidered on the back, surrounded by rows of pretty French ladies!

Sid slapped his hands across his eyes when he saw this. "Oh blimey!" he said laughing. "Save me, please. Somebody save me!"

Perhaps the most side-splitting sight of all was the double-act of Dr Reynolds and old Arthur Malcolm Cuthbertson, the Science Teacher. Reynolds had tried to maintain his dignity and pride by marching along, pushing his trolley with his head held high. He appeared to be ignoring the cheers, rude comments and laughter that were aimed at him. This may have worked, had two unfortunate things not happened...

Cuthbertson had obviously downed a tipple too many. He stumbled in behind Reynolds, but couldn't quite hold his balance. He veered to the side of his trolley, let go, and toppled forward with his arms stretched out. Grabbing hold of whatever he could, in an attempt to save himself further disaster, his fingertips hooked onto Reynolds' underpants. Creating the most marvellous ripping sound as he fell, Cuthbertson managed to tear the back end of The Bear's pants clean away.

Reynolds deliberately ignored anything going on around or behind him. He marched on proudly, trolley to the fore, his head held high. Now, however, a significant portion of both his posterior cheeks was revealed for everyone to view.

It was too much.

"My eyes! My eyes!" shouted Sid, covering them up again. "I'm blinded!"

"*Cheeky!*" remarked Arty.

"I *barely* recognise him!" added Soppy.

"Don't worry, Sops," joked Arty. "I'll get to the *bottom* of this!"

"Me, too," agreed Brains. "Have no *rear*... I mean, have no fear!"

Well things pretty much degenerated after that. The teachers got quite a lot of jip from everyone present throughout the rest of the evening. Laughing, joking, giggling and 'Mickey-taking' continued well into the midnight hour. Fruit Punch and Caribbean Cocktail flowed freely. Endless foods were scoffed.

But the real highlight of the evening started quite accidentally at around half past ten.

One of the First Formers knocked over a tall, thin Knickerbocker Glory ice cream. It landed on the lap of a Second Form girl, making a mess of her new denim skirt. The Second Form girl, Becky DeMont, returned the compliment by pouring a whole jug of double cream over the First Form boy, Craig Jacobs. Craig's friends screamed in fits of approving laughter. So intensely, in fact, that one of them threw up suddenly over the floor.

Craig saw the funny side of all this but now he wanted another piece of the action. He picked up his slice of jam and custard sponge and swung it round towards Becky. Becky duly ducked, so the sponge went hurtling towards the Top Table, landing on Big Tony Lincetti's face,

Tony licked his lips. What a lovely rich taste! Must be one from the local bakery! However, have you ever known a Sicilian not seek revenge? Still smiling, Big Tony reached over to the dessert trolley and picked out the largest fruit pie he could find. He took aim and sent it off in Craig's direction. Obviously it missed, but it did make contact with two fellow Third Formers, Alex Barnes and Rachel O'Hara.

It then became a 'free-for-all'. Everyone had been watching these exchanges, cheering each narrow miss and laughing at their friends' misfortunes when hit. This prompted others across the room to join in by hurling the contents of their plates and dishes. Sprouts, carrots, mashed potatoes, Danish bacon, tarts, jelly, custard, cream, mince pies, cakes, cookies from the local bakery, ice cream... Everything that had been on the menu became an aeronautical object lobbed aimlessly into space. Foods splattered into faces. Pieces of jelly gunged into ears. Custard matted into hair. Sprouts were flattened against the surrounding walls. Cakes and tarts crumbled over people's heads.

Worse still was when the teachers brought out a massive trolley-load of rice pudding. Cook had conjured up at least twenty huge vats of this, using nearly four hundred tins to produce it! The vats were shiny silver, nearly a metre tall, with matching silver serving ladles resting inside them.

So began the great rice-pudding extravaganza! It was the ideal texture – gooey, lumpy, warm and easy to throw.

As soon as Godfrey Mannering had dished up the first plateful, he had it squelched back into his face by Soppy. The plate slowly oozed off the end of his nose and fell to the floor. It left Godfrey in a thoroughly sticky state for the second time that day.

Mitch raced up to the trolley, heaved off one of the giant vats and returned with it to his table. Dipping one of his large paws into the vat, he scooped out a nice rounded pat. With a flick of his wrist, a wave of rice pudding sprayed over Sid and Fatty Balshaw. A second scoop sent a hailstorm over the next table, where Charlotte O'Driscoll was sitting, coating her with a nutritional blend of rice, milk, sugar, stabilising agents, guar gum and aspartame.

Everyone was completely plastered in the stuff. So, too, was the entire Dining Hall.

The teachers themselves had tried to avoid all this "childishness" – as Dr Reynolds had described it, but to no avail. They were the number one targets that night, so they got their fair share of pelting.

To top it all, Reynolds, Bannister and The Saint were singled out for some special treatment. Fatty had caught a glimpse of them out of the corner of his eye... tiptoeing towards the Kitchen. Fatty frowned.

"They're not getting away that lightly!"

He whistled loudly – grabbing everyone's attention – and pointed to the retreating staff. The children spotted them too and re-directed their bombardment accordingly.

The three teachers became sitting ducks and a concentrated torrent of warm rice pudding, cakes and cookies splattered into them.

Bannister decided that enough was enough. He needed a route out. He looked around... then saw it... the serving-hatch on the other side of the Hall. Bingo! He made a dash for the opposite wall, skating across the sticky surface.

Still the rice pudding rained down.

A few metres out, Bannister held his hands together and prepared to dive through the gap. Reynolds and The Saint watched these actions and decided to shadow his every move.

Mitch McGovern had, however, observed these actions too. He looked at the hatch, paused and thought to himself "Sebastian Bannister – about to escape? I don't think so!" Mitch studied the hatch and spotted a small red button on the wall to the side. It was the 'Open/Close' button.

Perfect.

He bent down, picked up a half-eaten apple and took careful aim.

Bannister was edging closer and closer...

With a swift fling of his arm, Mitch zipped the apple through the air... and caught the button full on.

Bulls-eye!

The plastic shutter began to close. Bannister saw the gap narrowing and tried to leap through it early. But his foot slipped on the slimy floor... he hadn't gained enough speed... he was losing his balance...

The children stopped abruptly and stared. Would Sebastian make it?

The ungainly Bannister soared through the air but reached his target just as the hatch snapped shut. The corrugated plastic gave a little, then bounced Bannister backwards. He collided into Reynolds and The Saint, all three collapsing into a congealed heap in the middle of the floor.

Mitch rubbed his hands. What timing!

He ambled up to the winded teachers. Looking around at the silent audience, he held up a vat of rice pudding... then poured the entire contents over the writhing mass.

The crowd roared with laughter. What a great way to end! Arty turned to them with a cup of Caribbean Cocktail. "To our revolution – successful in every part!"

The children were elated. They waved fists in the air and gave one final, conclusive, victorious cheer!

Chapter 10

Pay-back

It was getting close to midnight. Sunday loomed and things had quietened down. This was mainly due to the enormous consumption of rice pudding which was now taking effect. Blurry-eyed and all 'sugared out', the students who were still conscious were slumped in their chairs, chilling out.

Brains sat next to Arty and surveyed the scene...

The Dining Hall was a total mess, completely covered in all sorts of food remnants. Chairs and tables were scattered around the room.

"Ah, the spoils of war!" remarked Brains, sipping away at his diabolically sour Caribbean Cocktail.

"Yep! I never thought I'd live to see such a sight," added Arty. "I hope those wretched teachers have learned a lesson from their humiliation tonight."

Brains stopped to ponder.

"Do you think Operation Tixylix really *has* taught them a lesson?" he asked.

"No... not completely."

"I agree. It's going to take more than just a solitary evening meal."

Arty's eyes suddenly lit up. He clicked his fingers.

"Aaah! Got it!"

"Oh, yes? What might that be, 'King' Arthur Fox?"

"I think they need to suffer as we have suffered and in exactly the same way as when we suffered the most... during lessons! I think the teachers need to undertake a series of 'real life' lessons. But... reverse the roles! We become the teachers, they become students. Of course, we could add a few 'surprises' to their lessons. You know, spice them up a little."

"What an ingenious idea, Your Majesty!" exclaimed Brains, smiling. "A series of painful lessons aimed at developing their skills of *empathy* – the ability to understand how someone else is feeling. Excellent! Well done, Sire!"

"I thank you, humble servant. I take it that you, Sir Brains of West Mayling, would be willing to invent a few of these *surprises* for them?"

"Naturally."

"Lovely!"

Thus, a new campaign was born...

* * *

Sunday morning. Early. The seven friends were sitting quietly in the Staffroom suffering groggy heads and bubbling stomachs. Arty told them that very shortly they would have to channel their efforts and energy into creating a better future for their school.

He suggested that each colleague should come up with proposals for what they thought would be the best steps forward. Timescale: seventy-two hours.

However, before business comes pleasure...

It was whole-heartedly agreed that the West Mayling students should have just a little more fun at the teachers' expense. Arty and Brains explained their ideas about the pay-back lessons. Brains stood next to a flip chart and presented his timetable of the events for the forthcoming week. He told them how he had chosen the lessons, who was to take them, where they were to take place and what the surprise was to be in each one.

The others giggled and shook their heads. They saw another side to Brains at that meeting. They were all aware of his incredible knowledge and his unquenchable thirst for education, but they were hit for six by his surprisingly devious creations.

Fantastic!

When he finished, they gave him a twenty second standing ovation. Brains lapped it up with the biggest, cheesy grin ever.

The next item was how to inform the rest of the school. Another mass meeting was surely in order. But where? The tried and tested Sports Pavilion, of course! Time: midday.

They parted company and staggered out. All seven looked in dire need of soft, velvety toilet paper and a good supply of anti-flatulence pills...

* * *

The noon meeting was a fairly mild-mannered affair. This was put down, once again, to the students' inability to take their rice pudding.

Arty stood up and talked to the blank, bleary-eyed, sombre-looking audience before him. He told them how delighted he was that everyone had enjoyed the meal and festivities. He expressed his wish to keep the rebellion a 'positive experience'.

The one thing Arty had not wanted was simple mass rioting or the destruction of their school and its surroundings. That would have served no purpose at all. In fact, in his mind such acts would have lowered them to the level of the teachers! No, they were out to improve the situation at West Mayling, not to make it any worse.

Arty said that, if improvements were to be made, school life would have to return to normal. This was inevitable. "Lessons *must* continue as usual."

His comments received a few surly groans.

"But," Arty proclaimed, "these lessons won't be anything like as boring as the ones you're used to! They're going to be at least a thousand per cent better! And, what's more, there won't be any tomorrow!"

"Hurray!" coughed Barnsey.

"... Or Tuesday!"

"Cool," murmured the boys.

"... Or even Wednesday!"

"Wicked!" added the girls.

"Instead we are going to have a bit more fun!"

He then introduced Brains' ideas for the pay-back lessons.

This woke the audience and created a tremendous uproar. It echoed around the Pavilion, reminding Arty of the first mass meeting they'd had only twenty-four hours ago. He began to reflect on just how much they had accomplished.

Would the West Mayling students agree with the proposals? Were the 'special lessons' for teachers going ahead? Arty finished with a vote. Immediately, another forest of raised arms.

Unanimous.

Again.

Cheers all round.

It was set: the teachers were going back to school...

Chapter 11

Monday – History

First on the teachers' timetable was History, a subject "where the past comes to life," as Wellington Waters always proclaimed. He was a history man through and through. After all, he was named after the great Duke himself.

* * *

Wellie talked *really* passionately about dates, battles, monarchs, any historical event. This made his lessons quite interesting.

Then his sarcastic tones would appear. He always made students feel inferior to historical figures of days gone by. He said it was "their duty in life to admire the greatness of people like King Henry VIII, Richard the Lionheart or George Washington."

His favourite subject was the Industrial Revolution. He frequently declared that every student owed a "debt of gratitude to the inventors of steam power and electricity." These were the people who had made *their* "cushy existence" possible.

That's all well and good, thought Arty, but old Wellie wasn't doing too badly himself from all this ingeniousness, either. The thing is, he never mentioned that *he* should be grateful as well.

* * *

Bearing all this in mind, what should the teachers' History lesson be? A test on the monarchs since 1066? A study of the Spanish Armada? Research into the ancient Greek Gods? Or maybe an essay on the Egyptian Pyramids?

No.

No reading. No writing. No theory whatsoever.

It was to be a practical, 'hands-on' lesson. A re-enactment of the 'D-Day' invasions of the Second World War!

"What?" bellowed the Head. He stood shivering on the edge of the wet grass, just outside his office.

"D-Day," explained Fatty, "was the famous invasion of the sixth of June 1944 on the French beaches where the British and American Allies landed and fought back the Germans."

"Yes, I know all about the invasion, *thank you*," interrupted the Head. "But I'll be damned if I'm going to take part in a re-enactment! Such stupidity."

"Joining in is *not* an option, Godfrey," remarked Brains. "This is a lesson. It's on the timetable so you will participate. Full stop."

"Utter nonsense!" muttered the Head.

The children just ignored him.

"OK. You're the Germans – the 'Jerries'," continued Fatty. "We're the Allies. We've got you on the run. You've got to retreat through the school grounds, and –"

"Absolutely not!" cried Godfrey, defiantly. "You won't find *me* retreating from anything."

"I see. Well... that's fine," said Arty calmly.

He looked down and produced a mobile phone. "So... I'll just alert the local Constabulary, shall I? I'm pretty sure they'd love to hear what we've got to say about you lot."

"Oh for goodness sake!" hissed Godfrey.

"D-Day it is, then!" concluded Arty. "And you *are* on the run. Excellent!"

Once again his bluff had worked.

Mitch placed a chalkboard next to where Fatty was standing. Drawn upon it was a diagram of the school grounds. Fatty began to describe what the teachers' objectives would be.

"Right then, listen up. Your task is simple." He pointed to the chalkboard. "You're to move from here to the Main Gates. As you proceed, you must visit the locations pinpointed on your maps. If you make it to the Main Gates *alive...*"

Mitch sniggered.

"I mean... *if* you make it to the Main Gates," smiled Fatty, "then you have won. Is that clear?"

The Head looked unimpressed. What a fruitless task! Far too easy!

* * *

However, throughout the previous night the students had been hard at work. They'd made the school grounds resemble actual D-Day battlefields. They'd dug a series of trenches, a metre deep, constructed earth mounds and bunkers and erected miles and miles of fencing.

They'd even created the perfect atmosphere.

Brains had acquired a handful of canisters containing dry-ice. Where from? Brains wouldn't tell. He'd placed them strategically, so they'd puff out white smoke across the entire area. This created a low-level mist to float over the contours of the land and give the feeling of a real life field of battle.

It should be mentioned at this point that the trenches, fencing and bunkers were not the only devices to have been created.

Brains and Alex Barnes were Chemistry whizz-kids. What they didn't know about powders, chemical compounds, fungi or biodegradable products was simply not worth knowing in the first place. Their knowledge was combined with that of Charlotte O'Driscoll and her sister, Carla. Together, they came up with a selection of very nasty surprises tailor-made for their teachers.

First, there was the *'Barnes Bouncer'* – a bouncing bomb packed full of rotting compost. Second, a quick-firing machine gun – cleverly made from two ancient vacuum cleaners, which had been converted to use Brussels sprouts as bullets. Third, the *'Charlie's Angel'* – Charlotte's egg-bomb, which produced quite the most rancid odour you could possibly imagine. Last, the *'West Mayling Whammers'* – small but powerful, concealed water balloons filled, though, with yet more fresh manure.

These were all in full working order, armed and ready to go.

* * *

The adults huddled together in the dew.

Full of beans, the students ran off and took up their positions around the grounds.

There, they awaited the first wave of 'Jerries'.

The teachers started off in an effortless manner. They casually strolled along the pathway towards their first rendezvous point – the Football Pitch.

Suddenly, they stopped in horror!

They'd just had their first glimpse of the 'new' school grounds.

"My cabbage patch!" sobbed the Head. "What have the little beggars done to my beloved cabbage patch?"

"Blow your cabbages, Headmaster!" whimpered

Sebastian Bannister. "Look what they've done to my fields! What the hell are all those holes?"

"And why are there mounds of earth everywhere?" asked Devinia Longchamps.

"I don't believe it!" continued the Head. "They've gone and dug out trenches! When they said D-Day invasions, I didn't think they meant a landscape as real as this!"

"Trenches?" inquired Wellington Waters. "Why on earth would *we* need trenches?"

Wellie got his answer as soon as he asked for it...

The first of the Barnes Bouncers landed nearby, producing a colossal explosion. Heaps of dung and vegetation were thrown up into the atmosphere, scattering all over the staff. A second Bouncer arrived. It smashed into the earth, rebounded high into the air, arced back down and then became wedged – unexploded – in a clump of bushes close to the staff.

The teachers hit the deck.

The ground was wet and muddy.

"My new silk tie!" screeched Dr Reynolds in disgust. "Covered in dirt!"

"Well it's your own fault for wearing your pin-striped suit!" blurted Devinia Longchamps. "We were *told* to come in PE clothes."

"Yes, *Rupert*. Do stop that infernal grumbling!" shouted the Head. "We have more important things to think about right now, not whether your blessed silk tie needs to go to the Dry Cleaners!"

A third Barnes Bouncer landed just behind them, sending bone-shaking vibrations through the ground. The staff shuddered as they lay in the mud – heads buried in their hands, faces screwed up tightly.

However, lying there wasn't going to do them any favours. Godfrey decided that the best course of action would be a forward advance. They picked themselves up and darted for the nearest trench. In they dived, only to find even softer, squishier mud lining the floor.

Devinia Longchamps sat upright. Her face was coated with soil, her eyes with a pair of leaves.

Wellie had crammed his mouth with a kilo of dirt, 'Winston Churchill wouldn't have had to suffer this!' he thought.

Agnes noticed with interest that the texture of mud was identical to her chocolate sponge pudding.

The Saint was soaked. "Sacré Bleu!" he shouted, with a few more French phrases which we dare not translate.

That left poor old Dr Reynolds. He sat in a puddle, sniffling – his silk tie completely saturated and ruined.

The Head peered above the top of the trench. He gazed round the grounds through the mist and smoke the dry-ice and Bouncers had caused. He saw a few students' heads pop up at various points.

Godfrey paused for thought. Where were they planning to attack from next? He gathered his staff together. He told them: "The only way this ridiculous

mayhem will end is if we reach our planned objective
– the Main Gates." He knew the school like the back
of his hand. So he came up with an idea, one he
thought would out-fox Arty Fox.

The teachers agreed and set off.

His plan was to split the staff into three groups.
That would make it more difficult for the students to
concentrate their fire. However, Arty knew Godfrey
would try everything possible to escape another
defeat. He'd asked Brains to conjure up a few things
to counteract this. The sprout-firing vacuum cleaner
machine-gun was perfect.

Mitch McGovern took control of this article of
destruction. Both he and the machine seemed made
for one another. He stood next to Tony Lincetti and
Carla O'Driscoll, holding one of the pipes in two
hands. He aimed it towards the teachers.

Big Tony was observing the group of Bannister,
Agnes, Reynolds, Arthur Cuthbertson and Barbara
Alison through binoculars. He tapped Mitch on the
shoulder.

"They're moving to the right."

Mitch followed the directions carefully. He spotted
the adults, then squeezed the trigger hard. A multitude
of sprouts shot out of the pipe like flashes of green
laser light. They charged through the smoke and
peppered the staff as they ran. Some hard, some soft,
some mouldy, some smelly, the sprouts splattered
on to the fleeing teachers. Wincing as the sprouts

relentlessly caught their legs, arms and bottoms, the staff eventually gave in. They collapsed to the ground, covering themselves with their arms for protection.

Bannister produced a large, white handkerchief and waved it in the air.

The first group had surrendered.

Big Tony saw this, so he tapped Mitch's shoulder once again. "Victory is ours. You can stop firing now!"

Mitch smiled, "Sssh! Not quite yet!"

He carried on firing, getting both Bannister and Reynolds on the backside just a few more times. With a look of immense satisfaction, Mitch finally ceased. Carla grabbed her walkie-talkie and radioed Arty. Arty passed the message on down the line to Brains, Soppy and Fatty Balshaw. A minor cheer went up.

Then it was back to business.

They were tracking the second group of teachers: Dickie Howard, Wellie, Dusty Shaw and Devinia. They'd seen this group head for the left side of the fields where there were more trees and bushes. Soppy observed that, if the teachers managed to reach them, they would be a lot harder to attack. The bushes would shelter them and they'd be free to move. Then they could follow the outer wall back round to the Main Gates... and win!

Sid agreed. A feeling of concern rippled through the students. There was no way they were going to let any teachers win this battle. Not after the effort they'd put into preparing the grounds.

Brains had an idea...

He'd noticed the staff were approaching a line of trees with low, overhanging branches. These formed a curved tunnel through which the teachers could pass. Brains quickly explained his idea. They liked it.

Out came the Charlie's Angels egg-bombs.

The staff shuffled along, doing a good job of scampering from one mound to the next and from one trench into another. Dickie Howard couldn't move that fast, though, partly due to his 'dicky' stomach. He lagged behind the rest. Dusty Shaw trundled along reciting some Latin verb endings: "Amo, amas, amat..." Devinia tiptoed delicately as if treading on egg-shells but trying not to break them.

The students gathered up a handful of Angels.

The teachers were within ten metres of the bushes and safety!

Suddenly, they stopped. Had those pesky children spotted them? Seeing no students around – or so they thought – they made a dash for the bushes.

As they entered the tunnel of trees, Brains gave the order. "Now!"

Egg-bombs were lobbed high into the sky.

One by one, they looped up and arced back down onto the branches. The thin plastic phials burst on impact, sending a shower of evil droplets from the egg-bombs' inner liquid. The most overpowering, vile, rancid smell spread through the air. It suffocated the staff and made them heave.

Their faces turned green.

Then grey.

Two of them started to vomit in the bushes.

Dickie Howard dragged himself into the open. He pulled out a white handkerchief and waved it furiously.

Since *both* groups of teachers had surrendered, the staff must have been well and truly beaten...

* * *

The students gathered all the teachers together and encircled them like Red Indians around a posse of cowboys.

Arty smirked – yet another student success!

Suddenly, something struck him. Something wasn't right...

He looked round the staff and started to count... Abruptly, he realised his mistake –

"Where's Godfrey?"

Brains noticed Arty's anxious tone. Why was he sounding so worried? The enthusiastic chit-chat of the other students quickly evaporated. Meanwhile, the teachers' faces began to glow with smug delight.

"It looks like your little plan failed, Fox!" announced Dr Reynolds.

"How do you mean?"

"Well, we've out-foxed The Fox, eh, Arty?"

The staff began to chuckle in spite of their pain and weariness.

Arty scanned the horizon.

"Explain yourself, Rupert The Bear Reynolds!" he demanded.

"Godfrey, your Headmaster, will be at the Main Gates any time now. You see, his plan was flawless, whereas yours had holes galore. When we split up, we made *three* groups. Our two large ones and – on his own – Mr Mannering. He suspected that you would be stupid enough to concentrate on us. He knew he'd stand a better chance of getting to the gateway alone. You see, a solitary person can move unspotted, unnoticed. And he was right... you missed him! You may have won the battle, Fox, but it is we who will win the *war*."

Arty was speechless. Up till then, every stage of their plans had gone smoothly. They'd started the revolt and captured the teachers quite easily. Their demands had been agreed to without too much fuss or bother. The celebratory meal had been a success. Even setting up the pay-back lessons had gone well.

Now, for the first time, it really seemed that they'd been outsmarted.

Everyone turned to stare at the Main Gates.

There was Godfrey, puffing and panting, crawling, running, tripping over, then crawling some more. Only twenty metres from victory. Only twenty metres from a humiliating defeat for the West Mayling students. To the restoration of his power...

Revenge!

Sid swallowed deeply, preparing to face what had to be the fatal blow.

Only Brains remained unperturbed.

The Saint lifted his arms and shouted, "Victoire!"

Brains stepped forward. He was holding a small rectangular gadget. He looked The Saint straight in the eye. "Au contraire!" he exclaimed and pressed a small green button.

The button was located at the centre of his hand-held device. It sent an infra-red signal to detonators embedded in the West Mayling Whammers. These manure-laden water balloons had been buried in a line, directly in front of the Main Gates.

A series of eruptions followed.

Everyone gasped! The students with elation. The teachers in dismay. A torrent of slimy, cake-like manure rained down upon the Headmaster. He was halted in his tracks, encased from head to toe and stinking to high heaven. The students cheered, whooped and sang. The teachers hung their heads. Foiled yet again!

Godfrey stood motionless, hands hanging by his sides. He glanced down, scanned himself and sighed very deeply. He slowly pulled out his own white handkerchief and half-heartedly waved it twice.

Another huge cheer from the students roared throughout the grounds.

Once again, victory was *entirely* theirs!

Chapter 12

Tuesday – Home Economics

This was the girls' show from start to finish. It was brilliant through and through. Soppy co-ordinated it with the help of some Second Formers: Jasmine Archer, Becky DeMont and Gemma Hargreaves.

* * *

After their crushing defeat in History, it was feared that the staff might have become totally demoralised. They might give up hope, even revolt against the students, despite all that they'd agreed. This the children desperately wanted to avoid.

The teachers were going to get something a little more rewarding, more gentle, more relaxing... a spot of cooking in a Home Economics lesson! After all, what could be more refreshing than mixing and sieving, stirring and folding, baking, garnishing *and*, finally, tasting?

A course on cake and cookie baking was in order. This was mainly for Cook's benefit but it would also suit the other staff members. Thereafter, they might be encouraged to bake something decent for student snack-times, whenever ordered to do so.

Soppy had designed a lesson that would develop the teachers' ability to bake chocolate-chip cookies and double-chocolate sponge cake. You could argue that this plan was a little heavily tilted towards chocolate. It has to be said – chocolate *was* a firm favourite with the students. They were also sick to death of Agnes Brewer's 'creations'. Her fruit and jam sponge, for example, had never tasted either fruity or jammy!

* * *

Each member of staff had to wear an apron and a chef's hat. They stood in front of their workstations on which were a mixing bowl, utensils, various baking ingredients and a photocopied recipe sheet. It all looked very professional.

Soppy stood at the front of the classroom.

"Ladies and Gentlemen, today is going to be a chocolate day. Having miraculously survived Cook's attempts at mass poisoning over the past few years, I've decided that it's high time something *decent* is rustled up."

"Here, here!" muttered Dickie Howard, much to the disgust of Agnes.

"Yes. Well, thank you, Dickie," continued Soppy sarcastically. "Glad to see you agree. Just make sure *you* pay attention. I don't want your cakes turning out like your School Drama Productions: over-cooked, nondescript and totally lacking in taste!"

The other staff had to chuckle.

Soppy described what utensils were to be used, then the sequence of steps the teachers should follow. She started with a demonstration which consisted of mixing together some flour, eggs and butter and binding them together very smoothly. She was a complete expert. The Second Form girls watched in admiration of her control and technique.

Next, the teachers had a go.

What a shambles!

Opening bags of flour can usually be achieved by a four-year-old. Yet, apart from Barbara and Devinia, the rest managed to throw half the contents over themselves or the floor. Cracking eggs was another disaster. Most of the yolk and albumen slopped over the sides of the bowls or on to the work surface. By way of contrast most of the shells landed in what little flour they'd managed to get into their bowls.

Without his glasses Dusty Shaw couldn't read his recipe sheet accurately. He mistook '100 grammes' of sugar for '1000 grammes'. Without checking what the others were doing, he happily poured the entire bag of refined sugar into his bowl. He began to stir the crunchy mixture.

Soppy hoped he had a sweet tooth...

Arthur Cuthbertson emptied a packet of lard –

instead of butter – into his bowl. Soppy shook her head. Did he not realise he was baking a cake that would lay waste to the arteries of all who ate it?

To top it all, Sebastian Bannister poured half a can of engine oil into his cookie mixture instead of black molasses. He stood there wondering why *his* bowl smelt less like the sweet, sugary aroma of a baker's shop and more like that of the fume-filled garage of a back-street mechanic!

* * *

Two surprises, though, were in store for the staff. One was aimed directly at the Head, the other for the delight of them all.

Gemma Hargreaves had asked Charlotte whether she was aware of any exploding powders. Charlotte, being well versed in Chemistry, gave her a secret formula she'd read about. Gemma got straight to work. She poured it into a bottle containing condensed brandy and sugar, then placed it strategically next to the Headmaster. The bottle was simply labelled 'Brandy', so Godfrey thought none-the-wiser of it.

He poured the pungent mixture into his bowl and began stirring innocently. Gemma sidled up to him and engaged in a pleasant chat. She asked the Head to go through the exact amount of each ingredient he'd added to his mix.

"Young lady," the Head started, "I don't wish to

appear rude, but remember that you are talking to your Headmaster here. Don't you think that *I* would be perfectly capable of measuring out the required amounts?"

"Well... I *would* have thought so," announced Gemma. "However, I do believe that you may have added a little too much brandy, Headmaster."

"Too much brandy?"

"Yes. You see, if there is too much, when you put it into a hot oven, you'll find that your cakes will catch fire – or even explode – I bet you!"

"*Explode?* Nonsense, my dear!" boomed the Head, adding a chuckle at the end. "What a ridiculous notion!"

"Really, Headmaster?" scorned Gemma. "You're that confident? Go on then... bet on it... I dare you!"

She winked at Soppy. The teachers stopped and listened in.

"Certainly!" cried the Head.

"Excellent! Shall we say –"

"Two laps of the entire school grounds for the loser!" interrupted Godfrey. "At five o'clock tomorrow morning. Followed by a freezing cold shower!"

"Agreed!"

"Done!" smiled the Head.

"You certainly will be," continued Gemma under her breath. "Now, approach your bowl and drop a lit match into it. If there is too much alcohol, you'll certainly know about it!"

The Head stood with hands on his hips in defiant mood. He clicked his fingers and Devinia obediently rushed a box of matches to him.

Gemma began to retreat.

Godfrey opened the box. He lit a match and held it up for everyone to see. He looked around the room and beamed.

Gemma moved further away...

The Head dipped the match into the bowl.

The second it hit the secret formula, his mixture immediately erupted. A crumbly cloud of flour, butter and eggs smothered the Head's face and shoulders. He opened his eyes – two dejected blue stones set in a bed of white snow.

He said nothing. He was speechless.

The staff tried hard to mask their smiles. The girls roared out loud and cheered Gemma's success.

"You're a gem... Gem!" announced Soppy, holding the victor's arm aloft.

"*Eggs*-actly!" she sniffed. "It was a good *yoke*... I mean *joke!*"

"*Butter* luck next time, Godfrey!" added Sid, smiling at the Head.

* * *

As I said earlier, the surprises didn't stop with just the Headmaster. It was only fair that the others had their share of embarrassment as well.

This was accomplished by young Becky DeMont. She'd been to the local shops and bought some very strange powder indeed. On the side of the packet was written 'Methane-Inducing Mix'. When added to any type of food, this was said to produce a most amusing result.

Becky really was a little rascal. She always looked for the funny side of things and told jokes constantly. This often landed her in deep trouble, especially during lessons.

She wanted her revenge in a style that matched her humorous nature...

* * *

Becky had shown the packet to Soppy before the lesson. She was pleased and surprised to find that Soppy jumped at the opportunity.

"Methane-Inducing Mix?" inquired Soppy.

"Yes," whispered Becky. "More commonly known as Farting Powder!"

"Charming!" Soppy added. "Mind you, it's windy outside so it might as well be the same in here!"

Becky carefully laced the teachers' chocolate with the potent pink powder. She looked forward to the moment when all the cake and cookie mixtures had been put in the oven, baked, taken out and then, finally, eaten.

The staff broke the bars of chocolate and melted

them in a large saucepan. Dr Reynolds, though, was impatient. He chomped on a few squares of chocolate whilst throwing the rest into the saucepan. Becky saw him doing this and hoped he would get his 'come-uppance' for breaking her rules – just as she had suffered for breaking his.

No more than a minute after swallowing the lumps, the effects began to show. Reynolds tensed his facial muscles. He started to hold and prod his stomach. What was that strange feeling inside him?

Becky smiled. *She* knew what was coming next...

The other staff finished their mixtures. They formed them into little mounds on baking trays then placed them inside the ovens. The mounds looked more like 'splats' than sculptured cakes or cookies. Soppy shook her head a second time. These staff lacked any creative skill whatsoever!

* * *

Twenty minutes later, the cakes were ready for testing. Refusing absolutely to try them – with very good reason – Soppy encouraged the staff to "sample each other's cooking. You should offer praise where deserved, or advice where necessary," she declared.

Judging by their screwed up expressions whilst they ate, more advice was going to be served up than praise. However, they needed to remain as a united team. To avoid offending their colleagues, they just smiled, grimaced and politely swallowed their mouthfuls.

The rest of that lesson – in fact, the rest of that day – was spent with staff taking turns to rush out of the room. Just as hilarious were their phoney excuses for leaving. They'd dash off, red-faced, round the Kitchen corner or into the nearest bush. They'd return, still red-faced, for a few minutes more until their stomachs warned them it was time for another sharp exit.

* * *

Later, Soppy relayed her news of the day to the others. They rolled around the floor in hysterics, laughing so much *they* needed toilets, too.

"Oh, Soppy!" chuckled Arty. "You're a breath of *fresh* air!"

"That's more than you can say of our teachers!" laughed Soppy.

Chapter 13

Wednesday – Art Class

Art was a lesson that was going to be remembered for a long, long time. It was, however, not a lesson that the Art Teacher, Paul Pablo Durrant, would be in a hurry to mention on his CV.

Actually, the children were surprised to see him turn up that morning. Obviously, Art was his passion, so chances were he'd be there. But he was well-known for disliking official staff parties and any sort of meetings. In fact, Pablo Durrant hardly ever associated with his colleagues. He was your typical loner – shy, quiet, and introverted. He kept himself to himself and didn't bother anyone.

The children didn't view him as a security risk or threat. In fact, they really quite liked him. He was highly creative, helpful and harmless.

* * *

The children had decided that the teachers' observational drawing skills needed improving... as did their skills at being a waiter or waitress, their battle skills, their cooking skills *and* their general skills of tolerance, empathy, humanity, politeness, honesty and cheerfulness.

Observational drawing is a fine art to learn. It's one of the most important skills to get to grips with if you really want to develop your artistic talents. Looking at something closely, observing all the tiny details, then correlating these on to canvas – to the right scale and proportion – is by no means an easy feat.

So, that Wednesday's lesson focussed on 'still life' observation...

* * *

The staff sat in a semicircle around the wooden stage in front of them.

Godfrey was slumped in his seat, still rosy-cheeked and beading with sweat.

"Enjoy your two laps, did you, Sir?" goaded Arty.

"And your nice, cold shower?" chuckled Soppy.

"Nuts to the lot of you," snarled the Head.

"Now, now, Godfrey. Mind your language in front of the ladies!" mocked Sid.

Each of the teachers had a large white canvas, resting against a tripod easel. They'd been given a selection of graphite pencils, some charcoal and a palette of paint. In addition, they were all made to wear art shirts which were four sizes too large!

These art shirts were extremely uncomfortable and

impractical. But Arty insisted. "We've had to endure them ever since Nursery!"

"Absolutely," agreed Brains. "It is nothing more than 'developing the skill of empathy', is it not?"

On the wooden stage was a large cylindrical cage. Over this a huge cloth had been thrown hiding whatever stood underneath. Everyone settled into their seats and their discussions ceased.

Sid stepped forward to address the teachers.

"Today was supposed to have been a 'landscape' lesson. We had thought of sitting you on the terrace outside Godfrey's room to sketch the school grounds. We reckoned, though, that you'd had all you could stomach of the 'new' school features, trenches and craters included. So, if not 'landscape', it has to be 'portrait', doesn't it?"

"Where the blazes is Cuthbertson?" yelled Godfrey, looking around the semicircle.

"Oh – you'll see him soon enough!" remarked Sid.

Sure enough, Arthur Cuthbertson was about to be 'on view' to one and all.

Sid pulled a rope and the hefty cloth fell to the floor...

Teachers gasped.

Un-be-liev-able!

Arthur Malcolm Cuthbertson, the Science Teacher, was standing there... completely pie-eyed and naked!

"Good Lord!" shouted the Head. "This is an outrage!"

Cuthbertson was propped up by a wooden chair. He staggered and swayed, hiccupped and burped. Every so often he took a swig from his bottle of finest malt whisky.

Devinia took one look at this shocking, unpalatable sight and she fainted immediately. Barbara Alison blushed. She turned her head for a change of scenery and bashfully fanned her face with her hand.

Only Agnes Brewer sat there staring, completely fixated by the novel view. An enormous smile spread over her face.

"For God's sake, Cuthbertson!" shouted Reynolds. "Cover yourself up, man!"

The Science Teacher swayed a little more. He couldn't focus clearly upon who was yelling. He simply let out a lengthy belch.

"Ah!" he mumbled. "The fresh air feels good!"

Only the compulsive artist, Pablo Durrant, began to sketch the Science Teacher. He prepared a rough outline of the 'still life' scene, keeping well clear of the kerfuffle that was brewing between the Head and the students.

"This is one step too far, Fox!" ranted the Head.

"Oh pipe down, you highly-strung, old fool!" Arty slammed back.

"Don't tell me to pipe down, you self-righteous, young headache! Making us sketch this... 'naked Adonis' is *hardly* what I call a harmful prank! Look at Miss Longchamps! She's passed out because of you!"

"Belt up, Godfrey!" interrupted Mitch.

"Yes, Godfrey, put a sock in it!" added Brains. "You can stand there ranting and raving as much as you like. But... the last person to hand in a decent sketch of young Cuthbertson here will receive... fifty lines and a one-hour detention."

"Yeah!" cried Sid. "They'll be forced to scrub the toilet floors and eat one of *your* home-made cakes!"

The staff settled down and the lesson resumed.

Arthur Cuthbertson dipped further into his bottle of Scotland's smoothest brew.

The staff started to examine the Science Teacher in all of his natural glory. How they cringed and squirmed! Devinia had begun sketching Cuthbertson's hairy chest and flabby white stomach when she promptly fainted again. Agnes, on the other hand, was thoroughly engrossed in her picture. Eyes bulging wide, tongue hanging out, she spent an age drawing Cuthbertson's legs.

"Blimey!" whispered Soppy. "She's loving every second of this!"

"Yep," replied Arty. "Let's hope she doesn't become the next 'Naked Chef'!"

* * *

Godfrey Mannering hunched his shoulders and started scribbling away. He scowled and growled as he peered out of the corner of his eye.

"Oh, you think you're so smart, don't you, Arty Fox?" he whispered beneath his breath. "Well, watch out, because I'm not finished yet. I'll be back to get you, young man. Yes, I'll be back!"

The Head turned around and nudged Devinia.

"Wake up, woman!"

Devinia twitched from the sudden jolt. She looked nervously back at the Head.

"Wh-what? What is it, Headmaster?"

"I've had enough of this!" he snarled.

"Enough?"

"Fox has gone one step too far."

"Too far?"

"Far too far. I've got to rescue this situation."

"But, how, Sir?"

"Well, for a start, by contacting my 'connection'. I want you to arrange a 'session' for Saturday night."

"But if the children catch you doing *that*, we'll be in for the chop!"

"Good Heavens, *Devinia*," grumbled the Head, "just listen to yourself! You sound like a cowardly pupil. It should be they who are fearing us – not the other way round!"

"But, Headmaster..."

"Don't answer back. Do as you're told. I'm still in charge around here, you know!"

"How you can say that is beyond me, Headmaster. Look what you're doing – sitting there, sketching a bare person!" sniffled Devinia.

"I want none of your lip, *Devinia!* Now, make the phone call."

* * *

Wednesday evening. Half past ten.

Devinia wobbled into her Office. She didn't turn on the lights but fumbled around with the aid of a torch. She reached her desk, opened a small drawer and grabbed a black notebook. She ran her finger through a few sheets, then stopped. She'd found the vital number. She picked up the phone. Cautiously, Devinia Longchamps dialled.

"Mr Shanks?" she started nervously. "It's DL here, from WMH."

"Oh, yeah?" came the croaky reply.

"The... 'Servant'... would like his... 'Master'... to pay him a visit."

"Really?"

"This Saturday night? If at all possible?"

"Has he got what he owes?"

"Er... actually, Mr Shanks, I think he wants to... decrease his debt."

"Ha! So old Mannering wants a card game, eh? Well, he'll lose more money. Still, I don't have any problem with that. Count me in. Ta-ta."

"Very well," replied Devinia.

She delicately replaced the receiver and returned the notebook to the drawer. She stood up, crept out

159

of the Office and closed the door. Then she wobbled back along the corridor, her secret mission complete. Nobody could have known...

* * *

Soppy, however, had spotted Devinia's whispered conversation with Godfrey earlier in the Art Class. She thought it looked very suspicious.

Soppy said nothing, but had kept an eye on Devinia's movements all day. Later, that evening, she followed the jittery secretary down to her Office. She peered through the keyhole, observed Devinia's actions *and* overheard her phone-call.

As soon as Devinia had wobbled out of sight, Soppy moved in. She rescued the black notebook from Devinia's desk and took it immediately to Arty. It warranted close inspection!

* * *

"It *must* be important, Arty! You should have seen the way she was acting. She was even more nervous than usual. She's up to something. I sense it."

"Well if she *is* up to something," replied Arty, "it will mean that Godfrey is behind it. Devinia doesn't do anything without his permission. By the sounds of it, he forced her to make this call."

Arty flicked through the notebook. He looked at all

the names and numbers but nothing special seemed to spring out. He desperately needed a clue.

"What *exactly* did Devinia whimper on about, Sops?" asked Arty.

"Something about a 'Master' and 'Servant' –"

"Means nothing to me," shrugged Brains.

"– but she did mention a name."

"Can you remember it?"

"It sounded like... *Shanks*."

"Never heard of him."

"*Who* did you say?" interrupted Tony.

"Shanks... I think."

"Did Devinia say *Rory* Shanks?"

"No. All she said was *Shanks*. Why? Is something wrong, Tony?"

"Nothing... I hope. It's just that... *Rory* Shanks rings a bell."

Tony paused for thought, furrowing his eyebrows. He clicked his fingers and departed suddenly. "I'll be back in an hour."

The others looked a little surprised, but didn't say anything. They continued searching through Devinia's notebook. There was no entry for 'Shanks' but they did find 'Master'.

There were still not enough pieces, though, for Arty or the others to unravel the puzzle...

* * *

A couple of hours later, Big Tony returned. He looked troubled and agitated – that was right out of character.

"Where *have* you been?" quizzed Arty. Then he saw Tony's expression. "You look really worried, my friend. Are you OK?"

No reply.

Tony sat on the Staffroom table and ordered the others to gather around. He announced that he had some very grave news.

For the last two hours, he'd been doing research in the state-of-the-art Computer Suite. First, he'd had to reconfigure the school network system. This would allow him to link, via the Internet, to his father's PC at home. He started to explain what he'd found and why it was causing him such concern.

"The name Rory Shanks rang alarm bells with me. I thought I'd heard it before but I couldn't for the life of me think where. Suddenly, it came back to me. As you know, my father is a Judge at The Old Bailey. Well, at home, my bedroom is directly above the room he uses as an office. I can listen to the odd conversation echoing through the ceiling. From time to time I hear some really interesting stuff. Last Summer, my father was mulling over the case of a well-known criminal. Apparently, he was suspected of dealing illegally in stocks and shares. However, it wasn't just these crimes that caught my attention. The way he did it interested me far more. So, to cut a long story short –"

"Thank goodness!" interrupted Sid.

"– to cut a long story short," continued Tony, "I decided to tap into my father's PC and surf for information on his case. I found out that he had an unknown accomplice who he used for his illegal investments. Apparently, Police had observed this criminal taking regular trips into the countryside. These trips usually took place around midnight and at the weekends. Police were sure that the criminal was making contact with this mysterious accomplice, although they never actually found out who it was."

"Hang on a minute, Tony," Arty chipped in. "Is this story going where I think it is?"

"Probably, Arty. If you're on the same wavelength as me, then – yes."

"Slow down, slow down!" moaned Sid. "I haven't got a clue what you're on about or where you're both about to go next!"

"Nothing new there, then!" sniffed Brains.

"Actually, I hate to admit it," said Soppy, "but I'm like Sid. I'm not really with it. Can somebody please explain what all this means?"

"Yes, of course," continued Big Tony. "Sorry about that, Sops. What I'm saying is this. The criminal is a gangster called 'Hardball' Rory Shanks – *possibly* the same name that Devinia mentioned on the phone. Police suspect him of illegal investment in stocks, shares and other things. He has an accomplice, who actually invests his money for him. Shanks makes regular trips into the countryside. The Police think that this is when he visits his accomplice."

"Yeah, OK," nodded Soppy, "I've got all that. And?"

"And... the Police investigation found that this gangster had visited the area around here."

"What, near West Mayling?" asked Brains.

"Yes," replied Tony.

"Tony, I *do* know where you're going with all this," added Arty. "Do you remember those hot, sticky nights at the end of the Summer Term last year?"

"Vaguely," replied Brains.

"When I couldn't sleep?"

"Go on."

"Well, I swore that I heard cars being driven slowly up the gravelled pathway... in the middle of the night... at weekends. Don't you remember? I did mention them."

"Oh, yes," Mitch nodded. "I recall you rabitting on about 'cars in the night' for weeks!"

"Well?" Arty raised his eyebrows, wondering whether the others had yet cottoned on.

Silence.

Then, suddenly, Brains' eyes flashed wide open.

"Oh, my word!" he exclaimed. "You surely don't mean..?"

"It's possible," replied Arty.

"Oh Lord! This could mean trouble!"

"What does? What does?" yelped Sid.

Arty and Brains explained what they meant. Arty

instinctively believed that this gangster Hardball Rory Shanks was in the convoy he'd heard in the school drive the previous Summer. It made perfect sense. Shanks was dealing illegally in stocks and shares. He was using someone to do his dirty work. He took regular trips to the countryside. Arty had heard cars secretly entering the school during the middle of the night. Godfrey Mannering was embezzling the school money and putting this into stocks and shares as well. Devinia – of all people – phoned a person called Shanks. She talked about a 'Master' and 'Servant'. She asked for a meeting *next* Saturday night.

"Well, the 'Master' is obviously Shanks and the 'Servant', of course, is *Godfrey!*"

"I don't believe it!" gasped Fatty. "Please say it's not true."

"I wish I could," replied Tony, "but I think Arty's right."

"Why does Godfrey want him here?" asked Soppy.

"I think that Godfrey's at the end of his tether," said Arty. "I think he's planning some pay-back of his own."

"Yes, I believe so, too," muttered Tony. "I think he's preparing a counter-attack."

"Oh, blimey!" Sid spat. "We can't have this! We can't go through another battle, especially against a gangster. We'd lose! We might even end up dead!"

"Sid, I think you're panicking a little," sighed Arty, "but you're not wrong about one thing. We've got to stop this. We've got to act... now!"

Dark Times

Chapter 14

Master and Servant

What exactly did Godfrey Mannering have in mind by arranging for Hardball Rory Shanks to visit West Mayling that Saturday night? To quash the student uprising? To have a chat, a Chinese and a video? The only way they could know for sure was to confront the Headmaster head on.

But why let Godfrey know that they knew he was up to something? Especially when they could find out by quizzing someone who would be *far* easier to 'crack'...

* * *

"I honestly don't know what you're talking about."

"Don't play silly games with us, *Devinia*. We heard you on the phone. We know that Shanks has a meeting here. Why don't you stop all this nonsense and simply tell us the truth?"

It was Thursday morning. Ten o'clock.

Devinia Longchamps was sitting on her chair behind her desk in her Office.

So, was everything now back to normal at West Mayling? Not quite...

Devinia's arms were tied behind her back with some silk lace Soppy found in her knitting kit. Mitch had placed a lamp on the desk directly in front of her, with the beam shining straight into the Secretary's eyes.

The others were circling around Devinia, throwing questions at her, one by one. Though they gave the appearance of being very serious, the seven had to hide their smiles. It was all pretty amusing. Devinia was shaking like a leaf and they knew she wouldn't last long.

"You wouldn't want young Mitchell here to throw you into the outside pool, now, would you?" asked Soppy, trying to mask her giggles.

"No! Please! I absolutely *hate* cold water!"

"We know!" yawned Arty. "So – what's Godfrey up to?"

"Alright, alright, I'll tell you. But you're not to throw me in the pool. Agreed?"

"Fine."

"Very well. This is all I know..."

* * *

So there *was* a connection between Godfrey and Hardball Rory Shanks! Devinia proceeded to spill the beans. What she revealed stunned the seven West Mayling children.

Apparently, the Head was literally the 'servant' of Shanks. He was at the gangster's beck and call.

But why?

Unbeknown to anyone at West Mayling House – except the faithful Devinia – Godfrey Mannering, the Head, was in big, big trouble...

* * *

About a decade ago he was celebrating his new position as Headmaster of West Mayling House. He made the untimely error of entering a casino, which happened to be owned by Rory Shanks. Over-excited, over-confident, but a really *lousy* gambler, Mannering ended up losing the incredible amount of half a million pounds! Ten years ago that was a huge sum of money.

"Half a million quid!" coughed Big Tony. "How on earth was he allowed to have that much credit?"

"Apparently, a chap in the casino thought Godfrey was somebody else!" explained Devinia. "He made a terrible error!"

"I'd say!"

"But he paid a heavy price for his mistake. He was never seen again!"

The next day, Hardball Rory Shanks dragged the distraught new Head back into his office and gave him an ultimatum. Mannering had to pay back the money he'd lost, or he'd be forced to lose something else – his reputation, his job, or maybe even his life?

Godfrey was in a bit of a mess...

However... if the Head was prepared to do him a 'small favour', Shanks said he might be willing to lower the debt.

Pay back less money? A way out? For me?

Obviously, Godfrey jumped at the possibility.

So, what was the favour that Shanks had now proposed?

Devinia began to explain...

* * *

Shanks was a gangster. He was involved in a lot of dodgy business, most of which was illegal. He therefore had a lot of unlawful cash lying around. He couldn't simply pay it into a bank, because he wouldn't be able to explain where he got it all from. He didn't want to hide it in his mattress, as that wasn't very safe.

So what could he do with it?

The gangster came up with a plan. The answer lay in stocks and shares and various things like that, but he needed someone to 'launder' the money.

"*Launder* the money?" asked Sid. "What... do you mean Godfrey had to *wash* all his cash?"

"No, no, Sid," interrupted Brains, smiling. "Launder means you get your money into a bank but using somebody else's bank account. Because people think this person is OK, nothing looks suspicious. Then you can take it all back for *yourself*. This way, everyone thinks *your* money is legitimate, too!"

"Aah..?"

Devinia continued...

A colleague of Shanks told him that Mannering had a brother who worked at the Stock Exchange in the City of London.

That was perfect.

Shanks sat Godfrey down. He then explained the arrangements.

"This is what you're going to do. First, set up a new 'School' bank account. Call it the 'West Mayling Special Account'. I will visit you at weekends and drop off bags of my cash. You take *my* money and pay it into *your* school's Special Account.

You then contact your brother. You tell him to take this money from the Special Account and to invest it on *your* behalf. Is that *clear?* Your brother must think he's investing the money purely for West Mayling House.

Do not tell him where the money really comes from. Do not tell him about me. And don't ever mention your debt to my casino. Is *that* clear? We don't want him asking any awkward questions, do we?"

Godfrey shook his head.

"Let's face it, we know your brother's really proud of you. Newly appointed Headmaster of West Mayling House? One of the finest schools in the whole country? And *his* brother leading it forward, investing for an even greater future? Course he's proud. He'll be really chuffed. He'll be only too pleased to support you!"

Godfrey chewed things over. This huge debt I owe to a gangster? My life possibly in danger? Nowhere near enough savings to help pay it back? Not enough savings to live on, *if* I decide to run for it? My life *certainly* in danger! Now... a way out of this mess? Saving my reputation? Saving my job? Simply by involving my brother?

He had no choice.

Godfrey agreed to the 'favour'.

"You've agreed, right?" concluded Shanks. "That's your word of honour?"

"It is!"

"So be it. I'll lower your debt to four hundred thousand, but I still want my money back. So this is how we're going to play it. When I come and visit you and drop off my bags, I expect some pay-back instalments from you. I don't care how much it is, but you're not to miss a single deadline. By the end of each year, I *do* expect *at least* fifty grand back. Is that understood?"

Godfrey swallowed.

* * *

The casino debt – four hundred thousand – was *still* three hundred and seventy thousand pounds more than Mannering had! He knew he had to pay it off. Fifty thousand a year! And starting fairly soon! He

174

had to find an 'imaginative' way to meet his Master's demands.

There was only one solution: West Mayling House... his new school.

West Mayling was a Private School. Parents had to pay money to send their children there. In fact, they paid quite a lot. Mannering realised this was his *only* hope. He could use *some* of the school fee money to pay back Rory Shanks.

It was against all his integrity, his professional principles, everything education had ingrained in him. *And* it would break the School Rules...

But Godfrey reminded himself of the old saying, 'Set a thief to catch a thief'! In this case, to beat a gangster, he had to think like a gangster. Not only that, he'd have to act like one, too. He would have to break the law. He would have to become a criminal.

In other words, he would have to embezzle school funds!

* * *

"Poor old Godfrey!" sighed Sid.

"What do you mean – *poor old Godfrey?*" asked Soppy.

"Well, that explains why he took the school fees."

"Yes, but that doesn't excuse him, does it, Sid!" snapped Soppy.

"And it doesn't explain the staff parties!" added

Arty. "Nor why the teachers were having such fun. I mean... the clinking of glasses? The joke-telling? The expensive wine? It doesn't make sense."

"Come on, Devinia," pushed Brains, "how does this all link together? If it were all doom and gloom to start with, how come Godfrey was so happy last week?"

Devinia paused. She was stalling for time.

"You can't hide it from us, *Devinia*. We saw the party through the Head's window. Remember..? Last Thursday night..? Around midnight..?"

Relenting, Devinia continued the tale...

* * *

To get his hands on the fees, Godfrey needed a reliable ally in the school. Someone who dealt with the money. Someone who would let him get on with it. Someone loyal.

So who?

It was obvious.

Devinia Longchamps, the nervy School Secretary.

Godfrey knew Devinia was the key to his survival. She dealt with the finance.

He set up a meeting with her, but he didn't tell her the truth – in fact, not for a number of years! He said he had a brilliant plan. A way of making the money from school fees work twice as hard as just sitting in the school safe. He said that his brother could invest it.

The School would benefit so much. With oodles of

176

cash he promised brand spanking new buildings. "Think of the children," he declared. "How inspired they will be!"

Because this vision didn't fit with the old School Rules, however, Devinia was worried. She began to panic. Godfrey had to think fast on his feet. How would a gangster convince her?

"Miss Longchamps, it's a dream of mine to look after and nurture my staff. Like a good 'Shepherd', I must protect my 'Flock'. With the *extra* profit from my brother's investments, I will set up a lucrative Retirement Scheme for each of the teachers here."

He went on to say, "If you were prepared to bend the School Rules... just a little bit... and not say a word, I'll do *you* a small favour, too. *Your* share of the Scheme will be the biggest of all. So your retirement..." he charmed, "could be *very* pleasant indeed."

Got her!

Godfrey's persuasion had worked.

Devinia agreed to her role.

* * *

By mentioning the teachers to Devinia, though, he'd have to go through with it all. He would have to create a Retirement Scheme.

More expense.

"Damn!"

* * *

Godfrey started a small Scheme – but didn't inform the teachers!

He went about his risky business with Shanks – collecting bags and paying back the debt bit by bit.

After a few years, though, Devinia became worried – even suspicious – about what the Headmaster was doing. Who was this creepy visitor who kept coming to the school? What about her retirement fund? Why hadn't she heard anything?

Godfrey realised he needed to keep her sweet. The truth had to be told. He described every detail to Devinia – the Casino... the debt... Rory Shanks... the 'favour'.

Devinia was completely petrified but Godfrey reassured her. He would keep his promises. She *would* have a nice retirement if she stayed absolutely silent.

And she did!

Over time, staff inevitably left and replacements were obviously required. Godfrey had already planned for this. Right from the very start, he had only employed people whom he could influence, control and dominate.

How?

Through his own detection work.

He sieved through the lists of candidates and dug deeply into their past. He gradually chose a select group of teachers with some slightly peculiar secrets!

Shortly after starting their job, new recruits were summoned by Godfrey to his Office. He offered them the chance of joining a secret staff 'Club' – the very exciting and lucrative Early Retirement Scheme.

Praising their excellent work, he lulled them into a false sense of security – and then he dropped the bombshell.

He explained that it wasn't *quite* legitimate. If they wanted a cushy retirement, they had to keep their mouths shut! Forever! But a stark warning followed...

If anyone refused to join, or said anything about the Scheme to anyone else, Godfrey would make their lives really miserable. He said he knew "all their 'dark shadows' from their less than spotless past."

Being naturally greedy and fearing their secrets becoming public, the teachers all fell into line.

The ubiquitous West Mayling Code of Silence was born.

* * *

Utter shock. Total disbelief.

The seven children were speechless, to say the very least.

But they hadn't yet heard the worst!

* * *

Four years into the relationship, Shanks thought of a way to keep Mannering under tight control even longer.

Shanks was a gangster, but he was also a clever businessman. He could see that Mannering was an amateur when it came to handling money and so the gangster started playing games with the Head.

He offered Godfrey the chance to decrease his debt even faster. Gambling nights were arranged, and cards were played. If the Head won, the debt was lowered. If he lost, it increased. Unfortunately, the Head really was a lousy card-player. Shanks may have let him win to start with but, over time, Godfrey ended up losing a lot more money. By Christmas that year his debt had gone up to nearly seven hundred thousand pounds!

Godfrey was devastated.

He thought he'd be in Shanks' grip for the rest of his life.

* * *

Then, six months later, a miracle occurred.

Plodding through the grounds on one mid-summer evening, waiting for the sun to set, he received an unexpected phone call from his brother.

"One of your investments, Godfrey, has gone through the roof! West Mayling's hit the jackpot! You could be talking about two million a year... *at least*. Maybe even more – over time, of course!"

Godfrey fell to his knees in a state of total bliss. Am I safe? At last?

He sat under the great oak throughout the moonlit night – delirious, euphoric and mesmerised – lost in a world of possibilities.

Maybe, now, there was a way forward?

By the first morning light his thoughts had evolved into a stunning new plan. Tell Shanks the good news, but give him a figure that's much less... how about a *quarter* of the real amount? Five hundred thousand! He'll be pleased with that. Keep *three quarters* for other things... some for new buildings... and some for that damned expensive technology... about a million for those. Some for the teachers' Scheme... and what's left – over two hundred grand – for himself! He really thought he deserved it.

The sun burst above the horizon. Could this be the dawn of a new era? His freedom? His liberation? His redemption?

* * *

As the years rolled by, the money rolled in. His retirement 'nest-egg' grew. Not surprising, really. He started to stockpile almost two hundred thousand pounds *each year!* He increased his pay-offs from fifty to one hundred thousand. He even started to hold staff parties!

The teachers were happy.

Devinia was happy.

Parents were happy, too. Godfrey, they thought,

had established West Mayling as a centre of high-tech, cutting-edge, state-of-the-art technology with a wealth of superb new facilities. What a place to send your beloved offspring – despite the extortionate fees!

Godfrey still had to limit his costs, however. So the strict new rule was introduced that "no grubby paw of any grubby child..." was ever to touch the expensive stuff!

To enforce this policy he got to know the secrets of every single child as well as all the teachers. Godfrey's Code of Silence was now extended over *everyone* inside West Mayling.

Except for one... who he'd missed off his lists...

* * *

Godfrey was therefore the happiest of them all. He was close to clearing his casino debt. He'd really made a name for himself. And he was planning to retire in a couple of years.

Then a spanner was thrown into the works. A pesky young headache by the name of Arthur James Fox strolls into the picture and stages a revolt.

The rest, as they say, is history...

Chapter 15

Saving Bacon

Arty was stunned.

The others were stunned.

This was much bigger than they'd ever imagined.

They didn't quite know what to say.

For a start, they wanted to know if the Head was going to try to recapture the school.

"No," said Devinia. "All he's planning to do is clear his debt with Shanks once and for all."

"Why?"

"He's had enough. You've pushed him too far!"

* * *

Godfrey wanted to get out with as much as he possibly could. He was going to gamble *everything* in one last card game with Shanks. The profits. The fees. The retirement money. The lot! He was going to divide up the winnings between the School, the teachers and himself. Obviously, he was going to take by far the biggest share but no-one was to know that.

The problem was that he was bound to lose, which

would be disastrous. The School would be flat broke. The news might leak out. Staff could be jailed. West Mayling would have to close!

Indirectly, the students would be responsible! Their revolt was designed to improve their School not close it down! Maybe their pay-back lessons *had* gone too far. They'd pushed Godfrey over the top. They'd sent him running like a headless chicken, hell-bent on one final game of cards.

The children obviously needed to act promptly to stop Godfrey carrying out his hair-brained intentions.

* * *

They untied Devinia and let her go. Mitch promised that he would watch her like an eagle hovering over a field of mice. Should she mention any part of this confession to anyone, she'd find herself in hot water. Or, more accurately, in cold water at the deep end of the swimming pool...

That was enough to set off the waterworks. A tearful, shaky Devinia wobbled out of the Office and into the darkness of the corridor.

Back in the Staffroom, the seven astonished friends congregated to discuss the next step...

"OK. On Sunday, I said we had seventy-two hours to think of ways to improve things at West Mayling," said Arty. "Well, today is Thursday and the deadline is up. I reckon those plans are going to have to wait a while. We've more important issues to deal with right now."

"Yes, I agree," added Brains. "The small matter of Hardball Rory Shanks suddenly entering our lives changes things altogether!"

"But let's not forget Godfrey," chuckled Fatty, "floating around in his own little dream-world thinking he'll be victorious in that card game! That's what we need to think about first. He's likely to destroy any plans before we ever put them into practice."

"Absolutely. We can't let him get away with things that lightly," demanded Sid.

"Yeah, we've only pelted him with fruit, exploded manure and egg-bombs all over him, covered him with cake mixture, fed him Farting Powder *and* made him sketch a completely naked colleague!" smirked Soppy. "We've hardly had any fun at all!"

"I've got it!" yelled Arty.

"Is it contagious?" joked Sid.

"I'm serious, girls, I've got the answer."

"Come on then, Arty," said the others. "Let's have it!"

Arty took a deep breath. "Godfrey's in real trouble. In a way, so are we. Our fee money is tied up in paying back Godfrey's debt. The school is in the hands of Rory Shanks. So long as he is around, our school will never be able to move forward. Now, if Godfrey plays cards on Saturday night, there's a strong chance he might lose."

"Oh! Come off it!" interrupted Soppy. "He *will* lose!"

"Well... yes. We can't afford to take that risk. If he loses, our school falls deeper into Shanks' grip. As much as it pains me to say this... to save West Mayling, I think we'll have to save Godfrey first."

"Save that crooked old Crumbly?" whinged Sid. "Bloomin' eck!"

"We have to, Sid. Can't you see? Everything rests on this card game on Saturday night. We've got to give Godfrey an ultimatum."

"Which is what?" asked Brains.

"We take part in the card game. Or we go to the Police."

"What?"

"We play. We win the money. We pay off Godfrey's debt. Then we'll never see Shanks again."

"What's the point?" huffed Sid. "Sounds like more stress for us!"

"The point is, Sid, we will have saved Godfrey's bacon."

"So?"

"So he'll owe us a huge debt."

"So what?"

"Then we can demand that he puts all the profit from his brother's investments back into West Mayling House. In this way, our revolt will have accomplished everything it set out to achieve. No more embezzling."

"And no more Rory Shanks."

"Very good point, Sops," continued Arty. "Who knows, on Saturday we could win really good money!"

"And we could *lose* some really good money, too!" interrupted Brains.

"True. But not if you're an expert... like Tony!" Arty turned towards Big Tony and winked. "He knows every card game there is. He's been playing them ever since he was a wee nipper. He could beat anybody at any game, hands down. *I bet you!*"

Tony laughed.

"This is what I suggest," said Arty. "We confront Godfrey now. We tell him we know what he's up to. Then we make our demands. The gambling session on Saturday night still goes ahead but, instead of Godfrey betting against Shanks, Tony does it. If Godfrey argues or throws a wobbly, we phone the Police! It's that simple."

"*That* simple?" sniffed Sid.

"Yes. Tony wins and everything is sorted. Our success is bound in concrete."

"So long as *we* don't end up bound in concrete," yelped Sid. "I've seen those gangster films. They bury their enemies in motorway bridges."

"Sid!" snapped Soppy.

So that was the plan.

* * *

The others said they were happy if Tony was happy. Arty asked him if he was up for it. Tony nodded. Now they could put it to the Headmaster.

187

As you can imagine, no-one believed Mannering would take this lying down. That didn't matter. He couldn't refuse – he couldn't risk the police getting involved.

And so it happened. Arty and the others confronted the Head. A short, sharp conversation took place. Arty told the Servant that Tony would gamble against the Master instead of him. The Head huffed and puffed. How did they know about Shanks? Simple. Devinia's confession.

More huffing and puffing...

Arty managed to calm Godfrey down. He said the Head would still get *something* out of the night. They'd give him a slice of their winnings, but *only* if he agreed *and* did what they demanded.

Soppy reminded the Head what a dreadful card player he was. She said that *if* he played he would probably lose. That meant much more debt...

Godfrey frowned. He began to chew it over and paced around the room.

Suddenly, he remembered: the 17th Century Duke. Of course! One more Ace up my sleeve! Should I need it. If I *have* to run for it now! Something that *nobody* knows about.

Excellent! He smiled, beamed and agreed – which made Soppy very suspicious...

Arty ordered him to telephone Shanks to tell him the slight change of plan.

Godfrey had to tell a string of fibs. He told Shanks

he'd thought up an ingenious way for the Master to make more money. "It's all to do with the pupils," he wittered, "and their unbelievable amounts of pocket money. Add it all together – it's a fortune! I've managed to talk their 'Leader' into betting the lot in a card game against me. Then I wondered... would the Master like to take him on instead? I thought I'd phone and offer you this golden opportunity."

This suited the Master down to the ground. Beating a teenage upstart out of an unearned fortune seemed a doddle of a night's work to him. Shanks agreed without question.

Little did he understand the teenagers' ability to outwit adults!

* * *

Saturday night was set.

Godfrey Mannering handed over one hundred thousand pounds from the Secretary's safe and gave it to Tony for the evening.

Everything was going according to plan. The seven were delighted.

But, it still left one more thing...

Tony had to win against Hardball Rory Shanks!

Chapter 16

A Million Reasons...

Saturday evening. Nine o'clock.

The seven watched the long black Limousine pull up just inside the Main Gates. One of Shanks' colleagues stepped out carrying two bags of cash. He shuffled over to Godfrey Mannering who was standing in the shadows of the Main Building. The Headmaster took the bags hastily and handed over a thick brown envelope full of notes for Shanks. The Limo then proceeded towards the great Front Door, coming to rest alongside the tall, white columns.

There, Arty stood dressed as a waiter, wearing Dickie Howard's black tuxedo and Devinia's white gloves. He opened the huge Front Door and greeted the gangster boss.

"Good evening, gentlemen. This way, if you please."

Arty led the boss and his entourage of heavies through the Entrance Hall and into the Head's Office. Big Tony had set up a round table for gambling covered in smooth, green cloth with a low-hanging lampshade emitting a dull, yellow light. Tony was sitting there, waiting.

Their guest wore a very smart, slate-grey, pinstripe suit, with a red carnation in his jacket lapel. His shoes were shiny, his silk tie was smooth, his numerous gold rings sparkled in the dim light.

Shanks was completely bald. Although in his early sixties, he was doing a good job of hiding it. Arty looked a little closer... definitely a *fake* tan! A sign of age being covered up, he thought. Arty wondered just how many other secrets he'd covered up in his time... the threats, the blackmailing, the beatings. The torture? Maybe, the odd killing, too?

Each heavy was well over six feet tall – and seemed to be six feet wide as well. They looked as if they'd been carved out of granite. They stood motionless in their long black coats, arms crossed, looking straight ahead. They kept their black gloves on and wore dark shades even though it was warm and dingy inside. Neither uttered a word all evening. Not a "Please" or "Thank-you." Not even a "Can I have a cup of tea?" or "May I go to the toilet?"

Big Tony looked the part, too. Although he was in the company of Britain's most wanted gangster boss, he showed no signs of nerves. He used all the right gambling jargon and appeared totally at ease.

* * *

Half past nine. The first game of poker.
Tony dealt.

Just as planned, he started off by letting Shanks win. He wanted him to feel confident, become cocky... perhaps careless. Tony was sure it was the safest way to defeat him. Lull him into a false sense of security. Let his guard slip. Then go for the kill...

The best laid plans don't always go the way you want, do they? Tony had intended to lose two out of the first three games. But he'd lost all three! After losing another two, Tony began to feel slightly uneasy. Five straight losses. A trickle of sweat ran down his back. His tension now spread to the other six. They were bewildered, baffled and confused. What's going on here, then? This is definitely not right...

Big Tony had met someone who was every bit his match, maybe even more!

"It seems you're having a bit of a bad run, Anthony," smirked Shanks.

"Don't you worry, Rory. I'll bounce back. I feel confident."

Shanks looked at his cards. Two Jacks, two Kings and an Ace – very nice indeed.

"How confident do you feel, Anthony? Are you prepared to put *big* money where your mouth is?"

"Why not! In this game, if you win, you will also get... my holiday home in the Costa del Sol." Tony threw a set of keys into the middle of the table. Shanks looked impressed and nodded in accordance. Sid, however, unfolded his arms and stared at the keys. He recognised them... they were to *his* family's holiday home in *Florida!* Sid turned and whispered forcibly to Arty.

"They're *my* keys! He's stolen them from my room!"

"Don't give the game away now, Sid," whispered Arty. "Tony knows what he's doing."

"He'd better!"

Unfortunately for Sid, Tony lost that game as well.

Shanks laughed out loud and rubbed his hands in joy. He reached across and scooped up the money *and* the villa keys.

"Very nice, Anthony, if I may say so. Very nice, too! I can feel that lovely Spanish sun bronzing my body already! *Graçias!*"

Tony glanced across towards Sid, who was looking particularly hot under the collar. Tony wiped his brow and requested that everyone took a 'pit stop'.

"Too much Diet Cola, eh, Anthony?" suggested Shanks sarcastically.

Big Tony grunted. He stood up, walked towards the door, then signalled with his eyes for the others to join him in the corridor. Shanks said he needed some fresh air. So he went outside and promptly lit a long, fat cigar! The seven proceeded into the toilets. Sid shut the door sharply behind them and looked blankly at Big Tony.

"Jeepers, Tony! Those were my dad's keys to his holiday home! How am I going to explain that to him? He loves that villa!"

"Sid, Sid, don't worry yourself. I have it under

194

control. It's all going to plan. I'm going to start winning back some money now."

"Well, get my dad's villa back first."

"All in good time, Sid, all in good time."

"I thought the plan was to lose two out of three?" Soppy cut in. "Not all six! I take it that, this time, you *are* going to win?"

"Yes, thank you. I'm going for the jugular, but I've got to do it carefully. A few warm-ups first, then one big game. I'll bet the lot. It'll finish him off."

"Excellent!" said Soppy.

"Then we can end this creepy night and get rid of that maniac," yelped Sid.

"Oh... yes," mumbled Tony softly, "and the word 'maniac' reminds me of something else, too."

"What's that?" asked Sid.

"Well, can you remember when I told you that Shanks wasn't wanted for anything sinister?"

"Yesss..." said the other six, a little cautiously.

"Yeah, well, I didn't tell you the whole truth there."

"What?"

"You see, Shanks is actually *incredibly* dangerous."

"Dangerous?" gulped Sid.

"Yes," replied Tony.

"Why didn't you tell us before?" snapped Soppy.

"Better still, why didn't you get *rid* of him before!" screeched Sid.

"Because it would've looked too suspicious!" Tony replied. "That's why I let him win all six games. But I'm going to win it back. Besides, I saw a big, fat wallet hidden in one side of his jacket and a thick, brown envelope in the other. I reckon he must have brought an absolute bundle of cash to gamble with. Well, I want to win it *all*."

"Don't be greedy, Tony," warned Arty. "We only want enough to clear Godfrey's debt. Just gamble with the money on the table..."

"Yeah," interrupted Sid, "not with our lives!"

"Sid! Stop panicking. I'll win. Then we'll be home and dry."

"Home and dry?" muttered Sid. "*Home and dry* he says! He's just lost my dad's *'Spanish'* villa!"

The children returned to the gambling room. Rory Shanks came back in after finishing his 'fresh-air' cigar. The gambling continued.

Arty stood in the corner holding a silver tray. On it were cut-glass decanters of brandy and whisky, and a few elegant glasses. He served the drinks at regular intervals. Each time he approached the table, he quickly glanced at the gangster boss. He filled his empty glass with a shaky hand. He was nervous. He now knew the true nature of this man. He now knew the deadly consequences if Shanks thought he was being set up.

* * *

Knowing that Sid would be panicking about his holiday home forever and a day, Tony decided to win that back next... if he could.

Luckily, he dealt himself a brilliant hand – three Kings and two Queens – so Tony asked for the chance to win back the villa. Shanks studied his cards. They looked pretty strong. He nodded. Not only did he raise the ante to include the villa, he added an extra fifty thousand. He pushed the cash and the keys into the centre of the table.

Both man and boy displayed their cards...

Tony had won.

"Damn it!" snarled Shanks.

"Looks like that Spanish sun will be bronzing *my* body, eh Rory? *Olé!*"

Shanks hadn't taken kindly to Tony's words. He slowly placed his glass on the table, stood up, and walked over to Tony. He bent over and stuck his face right next to Big Tony's.

"The last person who 'took the Michael' out of me ended up being posted to his Grandmother... piece by piece. Get my drift?"

Shanks glared at Tony then sat back down in his chair. The room went silent. The seven West Mayling children gulped hard. Tony wiped his brow and said he needed another break. Shanks looked at his heavies and laughed aloud. "Public School fairies!" he mocked.

As earlier, the seven left the room and huddled

together inside the staff toilets.

"All going to plan, eh?" scoffed Sid.

"My plan *is* foolproof, thank you. Anyway, you got your villa back, so what are you moaning about?"

"Oh, nothing much... just the small matter of Shanks cutting me up and posting me to my Grandmother. That's all."

"Sid!" snapped Soppy. "Belt up!" Sid bowed his head. He knew his place.

* * *

Meanwhile, back in the Head's Office, Rory Shanks was sipping away at his whisky. Suddenly something caught his eye. It was a painting of a 17th Century Duke sitting on a white and grey horse, framed in thick gold.

But something felt odd.

It was hung slightly skew-whiff.

Shanks looked at it again. It was definitely not hanging straight. Now, to Hardball Rory Shanks – gangster boss and career criminal – this could mean only one thing. If a painting was not hanging straight, it meant someone had recently moved it. Paintings are usually hung and then left for people to admire but not touch. There would be only one reason why someone had touched it and that would be to move it.

Now, why would someone decide to move a painting?

Answer: if there was something behind it they wanted to get at. Rory Shanks knew of only one thing that people wanted to get at behind paintings on walls – a safe!

Shanks placed his glass down onto the table. He stood up and clicked his fingers at one of his heavies, who moved to guard the doorway. Shanks walked over to inspect the painting. He ran his finger along the edge of the gilded frame and smiled. He took hold of the painting and lifted it off its hooks. Although the frame was very heavy, Shanks was no mouse. He gritted his teeth and quietly rested the picture against the book cabinet.

Sure enough, there was the safe – a square grey box embedded into the wall. It was about half a metre in height and width, with a round dial in the middle. This was surrounded by very small numbers, rather resembling a protractor.

Shanks raised his fingers to his mouth and blew on the tips. He rubbed them on his lapel, gripped the small grey dial, then placed his ear against the safe door. He slowly turned the dial, listening to every click. First to the right, then to the left, then back to the right again. Each time a 'special' click was heard, he stopped and turned the dial the opposite way. After three special clicks, he heard a deep sound.

The safe was unlocked!

Shanks withdrew his ear from the safe door and stood back. He took hold of the small, grey, metal handle and jerked it sharply down. Another sound echoed inside and the thick door opened. Shanks smiled again, this time showing his gold fillings. He winked at the other heavy, who stood behind him, and peered inside.

Total astonishment!

There, in front of his eyes, were wads and wads of notes piled on top of each other. His eyes lit up as he realised that he was looking at a *huge* bundle of cash. Right there in the school safe.

"Gawd struth!" he whispered in his broad Cockney accent. "There must be close to a million 'ere! How the 'ell has Mannering got all this dosh?"

* * *

Whilst this was taking place, the second heavy – supposedly guarding the door – was looking inside the room. He was captivated by the wonders in the safe rather than watching Devinia's Office or the corridor beyond.

Arty was leading the others from the toilets back down the corridor. Just outside Devinia's Office, he stopped suddenly. He'd just caught sight of the heavy lingering in Godfrey's doorway. He gestured for the others to stop and held his finger over his lips. He heard murmurings from inside the Headmaster's Office. It was Shanks. What was he up to?

"Shanks is talking about *Godfrey* and his *dosh*,"

whispered Arty. "Stay here, I'm going to take a look."

Arty slipped to the floor and crept round behind Devinia's desk. He stopped just short of Godfrey's doorway and listened. He heard Shanks talking about a safe and whether he should rob it there and then. Arty decided to peer through the gap between the hinges and the door frame. He spotted Shanks standing next to the open safe. Then he heard a heavy ask "What's that, Boss? The Head's got a *million?* You fink we oughta nick it?"

Arty was flabbergasted! The students didn't know that Godfrey had a personal safe, let alone that he kept so much money in it.

He listened a little longer. Shanks said, "You bet! It's far too good an opportunity to miss. We'll come back later tonight and pinch the lot."

Arty reversed and crept back along the corridor to the others.

"Shanks is planning to steal all the money in the safe!"

"What safe?" asked Brains.

"Godfrey's personal safe. He's got one behind that painting of the 17th Century Duke hanging on his wall. He's also got a whole heap of notes in it. Shanks reckoned there's close to a million."

"*A million quid?*" screeched Soppy. "*That* explains everything! No wonder he gave in and said 'yes' to Tony gambling tonight. If it all went horribly wrong, he would still have this million for himself."

"A *million reasons* why he said 'yes' to us!" smiled Brains. "How are we going to stop Shanks from stealing it tonight, then?"

"I don't think he's going to steal it right now," Arty confirmed. "He's got nothing to hide it in. He was talking about coming back and stealing it later."

"Great!" tutted Sid. "Can't wait for that!"

* * *

Suddenly, an inspiration struck Tony. He clicked his fingers and smiled at the others. Without uttering a word, he strolled back along the corridor. He made his steps very loud – very obvious to anyone listening.

Back in the Office, Shanks quickly shut the safe and hung the painting back on the wall. He picked up his glass of whisky and turned round just as Big Tony entered the room.

Arty and the others soon arrived, still none-the-wiser as to what Tony had in mind. They stood around the room, flicking their eyes from one person to the next, wondering what was about to take place.

"Right. On we go. I'm enjoying this," remarked Big Tony. He dealt the next set of cards. "Maybe we should do this poker again! How about next term?" he suggested. "By the way, Mr Shanks, are you interested in Easter Fayres?"

The other six raised their eyebrows. The Easter Fayre? What was Tony thinking?

"You what?"

"Easter Fayres, Mr Shanks. Are you a fan of them?"

"Oh... er... yeah... I... er... love 'em."

"Wonderful. Our Annual Fayre is next weekend. It's a sort of 'Open Day' for our parents to come in and marvel at the school. They'll be able to see all our brand new equipment. You know, our expensive computers, the new heated swimming pool."

"Fascinating," sighed Shanks.

"Yes, they'll all be here in their pearls and furs, driving their new cars and spending their cash. The *whole* school is going to be *wide* open. There's going to be so many people here, we'll have to open up the *entire* school. *Every* room will be open to viewing."

"*Every* room?" asked Shanks, raising an eyebrow.

"Yes... every room. We want our parents to see absolutely everything that we have here."

"But not the gambling, surely, Anthony?"

* * *

Arty was listening very carefully to Big Tony's voice. He knew Tony was trying to do something – he wasn't talking normally. He was making certain words *very* obvious to Shanks. Was he trying to entice him to the Easter Fayre? He kept stressing that this room would be unlocked and open. Was Tony trying to persuade Shanks to steal the money then? It would be great if he were – as that could buy them some precious time!

If so, had he a plan to stop him? Even if Shanks put off stealing the money that night, they'd still have to face him the following week...

* * *

"Oh, no gambling, Mr Shanks!" laughed Tony. "No, the parents will be far more interested in other things. No-one will be wandering around this part of the building between two and three o'clock. Much too boring compared to the House Swimming Contest or the Modern Dance Festival."

"Really? Ahhh?" continued Shanks under his breath. "No-one milling around here between two and three? *Every* room open, eh?"

"Yes, well it has to be if it's truly going to be an *Open* Day. I, for one, am looking forward to it very much indeed. I think it's going to be rather *rewarding*."

"Yes, I do agree," whispered Shanks to himself, already formulating a plan to rob the safe. "It could be *very rewarding indeed!*"

Big Tony knocked back his pint of Diet Coke all in one go. He burped, then asked to be excused. He said he needed to answer the call of nature – again!

"Me, too, I'm bursting!" added Arty. They both exited the room, dashed along the corridor and into the toilets again.

"Arty, just very quickly... I reckon the Easter Fayre is the perfect moment to catch Shanks red-handed trying to steal the money. Who knows, we may even get a reward."

"How do you figure that, Tony?"

"Simple. I'll phone through to a few of my Dad's connections. I'll see if I can arrange something that will profit both us and Scotland Yard."

"I get it!" smirked Arty. "We're going to set Shanks up, aren't we? You're trying to lure him here and then have the Police waiting in the shadows to catch him. Is that right?"

"Exactly! Might as well leave the *dirty* work for the professionals!"

"Tony, apart from being an under-aged gambler of notable distinction and an out-and-out con-artist, you're really quite smart!" smiled Arty, patting his friend on the shoulder.

Tony tutted. "Gee, Arty! You're full of charm!"

* * *

Tony was about to leave the toilets when Arty grabbed his shoulder.

"There's just one more thing..."

Arty reached into his jacket and produced a deck of blue cards. He lifted them up for Tony to see.

"Our insurance policy," winked Arty.

Tony took hold of the deck and flicked through the first dozen or so cards.

They'd been rigged.

Both players would receive great hands, but one would definitely beat the other.

"Now, you've got to get Shanks to deal."

"What if he shuffles the deck?"

"He won't. He hasn't all evening. So I guarantee you'll get the first card and then the rest of the winning hand!"

"OK, Arty," smiled Tony, "but you forget... I don't need fixed cards. *I* can win the game myself."

"I know that, my friend, but we've got a lot riding on this game. In fact, *everything* depends on it. We can't afford to take *any* risks. Besides, if Godfrey is trying to 'pull a fast one' by hiding that million from us, I say we pull a stunt of our own. Serves him and Shanks right. Anyway, we're only conning a gangster!"

Tony nodded and smiled. A rigged deck of cards? Why not!

* * *

Both boys returned hastily to the gambling room.

Tony sat down. Arty grabbed a decanter.

Quite deliberately, he leant right across Rory Shanks to pour him another whisky. For a moment he completely blocked the gangster's view. With his free left hand, Arty delicately placed the rigged deck of cards onto the table. He immediately picked up the original pack, sliding it swiftly into his pocket.

He turned and winked at Tony.

The swap had been made. No-one had seen it.

Game on.

Tony was about to wrap that evening's affairs up quickly. He was going to go for broke.

"Your turn to deal, Rory!"

"Right! Don't mind if I do," muttered the gangster.

Without shuffling, Shanks dealt two hands of cards. Tony looked at his and placed them face down. He wasn't going to change a single card... with good reason. Shanks, however, decided to change one of his. A hint of a smile appeared.

"Right then, Mr Shanks. Enough small talk, let's up the ante a bit more. I feel tired and it's way past my bedtime. Shall we say winner takes all on this hand?"

"You what?"

"Winner takes all?" Tony pushed all his money into the centre of the table and threw the villa keys on top. "There we go. That's my bet. I reckon that, with the cash and my villa, we're looking at... three hundred and fifty grand."

"Three hundred and fifty... in one game?" coughed Shanks. "You must be 'saft' in the head, boy."

"No, I'm just tired," yawned Tony, "and losing concentration a little."

"Really... losing concentration, eh?" Shanks took one last look at his excellent cards. "Well, if that's the way you want it, Anthony, I suppose I'd better oblige." Shanks pushed forward his entire mountain of cash. "Right, let's see you beat this."

He placed the cards down one by one. King of Hearts. Fatty raised an eye-brow. King of Diamonds. Mitch raised both of his. King of Clubs. Soppy froze. King of Spades. Brains shook his head – four straight Kings! Jack of Spades. Sid almost wet himself – "*Four Kings and a Jack! We're doomed!*"

Big Tony wiped his brow and looked directly at Shanks. He copied the way Shanks showed his cards... slowly, deliberately, one by one.

"Ace of Hearts," he said.

Shanks raised an eyebrow.

"Ace of Diamonds."

Shanks raised another eyebrow.

"Ace of Clubs."

Shanks froze. One more Ace and I've lost.

"And..." Tony stared at his last two cards "a pair of Queens!"

Shanks thawed out. Only *three* Aces and *two* Queens? I've got *four* Kings – I've won!

Tony split the cards, holding one in each hand.

"Oh! Sorry, Mr Shanks. Not a pair. I meant *one* Queen – the Queen of Diamonds – and... *one* more Ace – the Ace of Spades. Gosh! That's *four* straight Aces and a Queen!"

Shanks gawped at the cards. Soppy, Brains and Sid gawped at each other. Fatty and Mitch gawped at the heavies, while the heavies gawped at the cards.

"I win. You lose!" snapped Big Tony, sharply.

Wow! Should you talk to a gangster like that?

Silence.

"Yeah... it appears so," said Shanks, calmly. "Well, what can I say, Anthony? Spend it wisely, won't ya."

He glanced at the 17th Century Duke. "It's so hard to hold on to money nowadays!"

"True, true, Mr Shanks," replied Tony, standing, "but enough of this trivial chit-chat. I bid you farewell. It's been a pleasure!"

"Oh no, Anthony. The pleasure *will* be all mine. I guarantee you that!"

Resolution

Chapter 17

A Fayre To Remember

The week leading up to that eventful day – the Easter Fayre – was going to be a hectic one. There were many things to be sorted. Plans had to be put in place. This would involve a great deal of co-ordination and organisation.

* * *

Sunday morning was a sombre occasion. All seven pupils had thumping headaches because of the night before. That made two Sundays in a row! Even so, they couldn't afford to waste time. The Easter Fayre was now just six days away.

What problems faced them this morning?

Basically three things. First, the imminent return of Rory Shanks. He would be back and he would want to rob Godfrey's safe.

Secondly, the Fayre itself. How were they going to combine sorting out Rory Shanks whilst hosting an action-packed, fun-filled day? And what about the school grounds? They were in a bit of a state!

Then, thirdly, the million pounds in the safe. What if Godfrey decided to remove the money or even scarper with it before next weekend? What could they do about that?

* * *

First, Rory Shanks. How to stop *him* getting the dosh? After much deliberation, the seven decided they wouldn't be able to tackle him alone. He was a gangster, a hardened criminal. And he'd be accompanied, no doubt, by his enormous heavies. All in all, he was way out of their league. They needed the help of the Police. Tony was given the job of contacting them because his father had 'connections'. But the students didn't want the police to contact Godfrey. Godfrey wasn't to know anything about Shanks' return. So the phone-call had to be left to the last minute – very late on Friday.

The students also wanted to keep the arrest low-key. As they'd already discussed, they didn't want their revolt to hit the headlines. No-one was to know about it, nor the pay-back lessons, nor Godfrey's dark secrets, nor their gambling. They simply wanted the Police in, the arrest made, then the Police to leave quietly.

Secondly, arranging the Fayre. What should the events be? What order should they be in? A typical run-of-the-mill Fête wouldn't do! The children wanted a Fayre to end all Fayres: numerous stalls, interesting games, spectacular events and record numbers of parents attending. However, whatever the numbers, parents had to be diverted away from Shanks, the safe, in fact the whole Main Building between two and three o'clock.

"Isn't that when the House Swimming Contest is on – followed by the First Formers' Modern Dance Festival?" asked Fatty.

"That's right," said Soppy.

"That's hardly going to set the world on fire!" moaned Sid.

"How do you mean, Sid?"

"Well, if it's a hot day, the parents won't want to be indoors watching the swimming. And not all the parents will be interested in *Modern Dance!*"

"For once, Sid, you're absolutely right," agreed Soppy.

"That makes a change," muttered Brains.

"So what will appeal to *everyone?*" probed Arty.

"I've got the perfect solution," snapped Mitch. "A fast and furious Staff versus Students Hockey Match."

"How about a Dance performance by the teachers, instead?" suggested Soppy.

"Excellent!" said Arty. "You won't be too upset if we don't include *all* the teachers, though, will you?"

"Why? What have you got in mind, Arty?"

"A solo performance. Let's just leave it at that!"

"That's fine," Brains concluded. "But whatever you decide, all information has to be given to Fatty by three o'clock this afternoon. He's got to redesign and print new flyers today, then post them first thing Monday morning.

Next they thought about the school grounds. They had to be re-structured.

There were quite a few scars left over from the revolt and the pay-back lessons. These had to be removed before the Fayre. The trenches and bunkers had to be filled in. The earth mounds had to be shifted. Fencing had to be pulled up.

The children reckoned that these would all be difficult tasks.

What was their solution?

Easy! Common sense told them to get the teachers to do it!

Thirdly, the one million pounds in the safe. No-one argued with Arty when he put forward the notion that it belonged to West Mayling House. It should go back into School funds. That should make up for the fee money that Godfrey had embezzled over the years.

Supposing Godfrey decided to remove it now, or worse still, do a runner with it over the next few days? Brains had a simple solution.

"I'll change the combination. Give me about five minutes!"

"Can you do that, Brains?" asked Arty.

"Naturally," sniffed Brains.

"Really! You're a constant source of amazement, my friend!"

"Naturally," sniffed Brains.

* * *

Monday morning. Five days to go to the Fayre.

School life was gradually returning to normal, but a forbidding threat hung over the teachers. If they didn't perform a *thousand* per cent better than they'd done before the rebellion, they'd find themselves back in lessons again. This was a prospect they certainly didn't relish and it became evident fairly soon that the threat had sunk in. Nothing untoward happened.

That, though, hadn't stopped the problem of 'wind'. Becky DeMont's Farting Powder had certainly done its trick, only its effects had lasted a whole lot longer than the girls originally expected. Dr Reynolds, the unloved Maths Teacher, was caught out the worst, to the delight of many students.

It was quarter past nine and the Third Form Maths lesson had just started. The Bear was dazzling his audience. The children sat in a state of shock. He was full of energy, presenting 'Problem Solving' with so much enthusiasm and passion, the students thought he might burst.

Then it started. Out of the blue, they all heard a small squeak. It shattered the trance. Everyone looked round at each other. The Bear, though, carried on regardless, totally engrossed in his exciting, new, teaching style.

A few minutes later, another vibrating 'raspberry' sound was noticed, followed shortly by a very uncouth odour! The children started questioning or accusing their friends of having 'dealt' the offending whiff. Everyone denied it totally.

Suddenly, a third, much louder 'trump' erupted, thundering around the room. It *had* to be The Bear!

* * *

Thursday morning. Two days to go in which to clean up the buildings and clear up the grounds.

Eight o'clock. Arty announced the start of the school 'make-over'.

It was the teachers' duty to do all the donkey-work. Carpets needed hoovering. Rice-pudding needed scraping off the Dining Room floor. The cabinets in every room, office and classroom needed dusting. The school trophies needed bending back into shape and polishing. The Trophy Cabinet needed mending and fixing back onto the wall. Windows needed cleaning. Certain window frames needed repainting...

Teachers were finished by sundown. They were permitted a solitary glass of beer and then it was straight to bed. For tomorrow the *real* hard work commenced!

* * *

Friday. One day to go.

Six o'clock in the morning. A gang of weary teachers reported for duty outside Godfrey's Office.

As well as repairing the D-Day battle-fields, the staff were dished out a list of other chores.

The school lawns and fields needed cutting. The football, rugby and hockey pitches needed their lines repainted. The swimming pools needed the chlorine changed. The showers and toilets needed bleaching. The outer walls surrounding the school grounds needed the moss scraped off them. Finally, the school shield on the Main Gates needed buffing up.

By six o'clock in the evening, the teachers were completely exhausted. Due to their tireless efforts, however, West Mayling House was once more a spectacle to behold.

* * *

Friday. Seven o'clock in the evening.

Devinia's Office.

Big Tony made the crucial phone call. His father knew all the top officials at Scotland Yard. So Tony knew who to inform and what he had to say.

He obviously couldn't mention that he was the son of Alessandro Lincetti. Nor could he say he was a student who'd just conned Shanks out of hundreds of thousands of pounds. Nor blurt out anything about the Headmaster, the staff or the embezzlement of cash. And, obviously, nothing whatsoever to do with the revolt!

No. He had to think of another way...

"Is that the Superintendent at Scotland Yard?" he started, in a very deep, croaky voice.

"Yes, this is the *Detective Chief* Superintendent Benjamin talking. And my Sergeant here informs me you have something to say about... Rory Shanks?"

"That is correct, yes. I am a member of his crime organisation."

"Are you indeed? So, you're what we call a 'Grass' then? An informer, who tells tales from the inside?" asked the Chief.

"Whatever," sniffed Tony. "Now, just listen carefully. Shanks will be at West Mayling House tomorrow, Saturday. He's planning to rob the school safe."

"Oh, yes?" inquired the Chief, a little amused at hearing this. "And what's he going to steal? The exam results and a bit of French homework!"

"That's very funny, Chief. You should be on the telly," continued Big Tony. "Do you want Shanks or do you not?"

"We do," answered the Chief, "but why is he going to West Mayling House?"

"There's a hundred grand sitting in their safe. He's gonna rob it. He wants to nick the lot. Well it's out of order, that – stealing from kids."

"One hundred thousand, eh? It's a bit silly, keeping that amount in a school safe!"

"That's not the issue right now, is it Chief? The main point is, do you want Shanks or not?"

"We do."

"Good... Just be outside West Mayling around two-thirty on Saturday. Then I want you to storm in at *exactly* two-forty. No earlier. No later. Do you understand? Two-forty. No earlier. No later."

The Detective Chief Inspector agreed. He then tried to get more information from Tony. Tony didn't want to let the cat out of the bag by saying something he shouldn't, so he put the phone down immediately. He certainly didn't want the Police to know the truth – that there was a million pounds sitting comfortably in Godfrey's safe. The students wanted that to go straight back into the school where it belonged.

Soppy looked suitably impressed by Big Tony's performance. She gave him a 'thumbs up'. Brains and Sid were also in the Office, whilst Mitch stood guard in the doorway.

"Do you think it will work, Tony?" she asked.

"I think so," he replied, nodding his head. "They want him badly enough. They'll be here tomorrow."

"What's stopping them coming tonight and ruining things?" asked Sid.

"No, I don't think they'll do that," continued Big Tony. "They're *very* smart, Sid. They'll do it properly. They'll turn up tomorrow without anyone noticing them. You'll see. They'll probably do a stake-out on some of the surrounding roads. They'll certainly keep a close eye on the entrance at the Main Gates, but that's all."

"So," said Brains, "we must be on high alert. Let's not get caught out. Everything has got to go like clockwork tomorrow. I've worked the details out to the exact second. It will all run smoothly and on time. That I assure you."

"Mitch," continued Tony, "have you got something sorted for those heavies?"

"Oh, yes!" grinned Mitch. "It will be quick and painless!"

"Really? Painless?"

"Well... no. Actually, very painful indeed. I lied about that part."

"Splendid."

* * *

Eight o'clock. Arty was sitting next door, behind the Headmaster's desk, feet up, reading a comic book. Godfrey Mannering burst through the door clutching a flyer advertising the Easter Fayre to their parents.

"Just what do you think you're playing at, Fox?" boomed Godfrey.

"Reading," replied Arty contemptuously. "So keep it down."

"Not that... *this!* I've only just seen *this*." The Head

thrust the new flyer towards Arty. "What the dickens do you call *this?*"

"A piece of paper."

The Head tapped the flyer. "I mean, what's *on* the paper!"

"What? The ink?"

"Not the ink, you fool. The writing, the writing!"

Arty took the sheet off the Head and pretended to scan through it. "The Annual Easter Fayre will be held on Saturday, April the..."

"I'm not interested in the date, you clown! It's *these* damned things, these new events you've concocted that are bothering me!"

"What? The Welly-Wanging Competition? Or the Flan-Eating Contest?"

"Not those," interrupted the Head. He stepped forward. "These changes, here!"

"Oh!" grinned Arty. "You mean the Hockey Match and the Ballet."

"Damn right I do! Particularly this 'Ballet' nonsense."

"What's wrong with it?"

"You know perfectly well what's wrong with it. Every year we have a Modern Dance Festival. It's the highlight of the Fayre. This year was supposed to be for First Formers. Now, it says... *Swan Lake... to be performed by a guest Ballerina.*"

"And?"

"*Don't* think *I* don't know who you've got in mind for that!"

"Oh, I dunno... thought you might look nice in a pink tutu. Anyway, serves you right for making us save your bacon. Spending last Saturday night with Rory Shanks was not the most pleasant of experiences, I can tell you!"

"No!" cried the Head, defiantly. "Absolutely not! I *won't* do it! Do you hear me? I simply *won't* do it!"

Arty stood up and leant on the desk. "You'll do it, Godfrey, or you'll go to jail. Let's get one thing straight. You don't like me and I don't like you. Just remember, though, both you and the teachers are still under a rebellion here. We're going to sort things out at West Mayling. You're going to do as you're told. You're lucky your backside isn't sitting in the local 'slammer' at the moment on a charge of mass-embezzlement! That goes for your pathetic staff as well. So, if I say you'll do a ballet performance dressed in a pink tutu, then a ballet performance in a pink tutu you shall do!"

"You're a lunatic, Fox!" raved the Head, waving his finger at Arty. "Do you hear? A lunatic! It's *you* that belongs in jail, not *me!*"

"Nuts! Listen, Godfrey. Don't think for one minute that we haven't got everything worked out, because we have. We're even offering you a respectable departure from here *and* a pension to boot."

"Pension? What the hell do you mean – a pension? I've already got a pension!"

"Not for long, you haven't – not if you carry on in *that* tone."

"Oh, for goodness sake. Very well. I'm listening."

"About time. Right, first, we're going to pay off your debt to Shanks. This isn't for you, by the way. We're doing it for West Mayling. To get him off your back, we *guarantee* that he'll be in jail within seven days. We're going to give you fifty thousand to keep your mouth shut and bow out graciously – *this* year. We'll pay twenty thousand to each teacher, too, but we're going to insist on a few resignations as well. Agreed?"

* * *

The Head thought for a second. Should he scarper now? Should he not just take his million pounds from his safe and get out before being humiliated in front of the parents? Wisely, he stopped to ponder the situation.

If he made a run for it, he'd never find peace. The children, and possibly Devinia, would spill the beans on him. They'd tell the Police about his fraudulent past. The Police would come after him. They'd hunt him down wherever he lived. He'd probably end up in prison for a very long time to come. And Shanks could still want all his *laundered* money back, as well.

Why bother running?

In his eyes, things were going well. Yes, those pesky pupils had just saved his bacon. They'd cleared his debt with Rory Shanks, who the children promised would soon be in jail. So Shanks could *never* hassle him for the laundered money he'd invested through his brother.

Only Devinia knew about the gangster – no other adults. She'd never say anything. Thinking about her retirement fund would seal her lips for good. So his reputation was intact there.

The teachers' Retirement Scheme was blossoming. Five years of good savings had gone into that pot. Each teacher was going to receive a very healthy pay-off next year. They're going to be more than happy. They'll think he's a star. So, reputation intact there, too.

On top of all that, he'd stockpiled his secret stash of cash – the million pounds in his safe – which, he thought, *absolutely* no-one knew about. Why not grit his teeth and wait? Why not perform the ballet and keep those pupils happy? Life is returning to normal around the school. He could see through the rest of this year, officially retire at the end of the Summer Term and live a life of comfort in the Caribbean.

He'd be hailed a genius by his brother, a good shepherd by his flock, a sweetie by Devinia, and a legend by the parents. Who cares what a bunch of self-righteous young pupils think? Anyway, they were even prepared to give him another fifty thousand! For ten minutes ballet? More fool them!

So, no. Don't scarper. Agree to the ballet, but don't make it look too obvious. Play for time. Barter a bit...

* * *

"Two hundred thousand!"

"*What?* One twenty-five and not a penny more. Not that you deserve a single pound of it, you crooked old degenerate!"

Godfrey thought for a second – 'another seventy-five thousand?' He quickly agreed. "Done!"

"You certainly have been," sniffed Arty. "But if you so much as cough out of line or if you sneeze at the wrong moment then the deal's off. Do you understand, Godfrey?"

"Nuts!" came the reply.

Chapter 18

Gangster Rap Ballet

Saturday. The big day.

The Easter Fayre was upon them.

Things *had* to go to plan right from the start. At seven o'clock, the grounds were already bustling with the sound of stalls being erected. Teams of joyous First Form girls and boys were preparing all the food. Cakes, cookies, buns, tarts, flans, meringues and sandwiches were being created in the Kitchens.

* * *

Eight o'clock.

Brains gathered the other six together in the Old Library. He wanted to check things one final time.

"Right, let's go through the timetable again. Split-second timing is extremely important. I shouldn't have to remind you of that –"

"But of course you will, anyway," interrupted Sid, sarcastically.

"Sid!" snapped Soppy, "Button it! This is important!"

Brains continued.

"We've told Shanks that this part of the school will be empty between two and three o'clock. If he's not a complete spanner, he's bound to rob the safe then. Don't forget – all the teachers and all the parents *absolutely have* to be occupied between those hours. However, we daren't set up Godfrey's Office before two o'clock just in case any teachers or parents stumble in and discover us. That would be a disaster.

So, first, we must get everyone to the Hockey Pitch *before* two o'clock. Blankets will be on the PA system. He'll announce when the game is about to start. Charlotte's teams of First and Second Formers will... *encourage* people away from the stalls to the Match."

"*Encourage?*" questioned Sid.

"Yes," replied Brains. "The teams will basically march everyone very quickly to the Match... using subtle force if necessary."

"*Subtle force?*" queried Sid.

"Time is of the essence, Sid! We can't afford to waste any! We need to get them there fast. Once there, it's vital that *you*, Fatty, keep in contact with Arty and myself when we're working in Godfrey's Office. Have you checked your ear-piece?"

"Yep! Receiving you loud and clear!" replied Fatty smiling.

"Good. Then keep us up to date... when the parents arrive... when the Match starts... all that sort of thing."

"Very well. But won't you be able to see everything through the webcam?"

"Well... yes," boasted Brains. "I'm going to set up a number of webcams around the school. There's going to be one on the Main Gates so I can see when Shanks arrives. There will be another on the great oak overlooking the Hockey Pitch to make sure the game goes sweetly. Next, I will place one inside the Main Hall to watch Godfrey's epic performance. Lastly, at two o'clock, I'll be setting up two CCTV cameras downstairs. One will be in between Devinia's Office and the corridor filming the Front Door and the Entrance Hall. The other will be in between Devinia's Office and Godfrey's so we can film Shanks robbing the safe."

"Brilliant!" smiled Soppy. "Well done, Brains!"

"I thank you. But cameras alone won't win us the day. We will have to be on top form, too. We must stay vigilant. We must be in control. We *must* make everything work."

"Absolutely," agreed Arty. The others nodded in accordance.

"Good. So... next?" Brains glanced down at his list of actions. "Whilst Mitch and the others beat the teachers at Hockey, Arty and I will finish setting up Godfrey's Office. Mitch, don't forget that you've got to make the Match *so* exciting that all the spectators stay there for *at least* thirty minutes."

"Sure thing, Boss," saluted Mitch.

"When the Match is finished, the parents will be *encouraged* by the First and Second Form teams to make their way speedily into the Main Hall for Godfrey's ballet performance. There mustn't be *any* stragglers left lingering around... the grounds, the stalls... anywhere.

It will be just after two-thirty at this point. Soppy, Sid, this is where you come in. Make sure everything goes to plan with the performance. Once everyone's in the Hall, *no-one* is to leave for at least *twenty* minutes. You've got to keep Godfrey going."

"OK," replied Soppy.

"Are your ear-pieces working?"

"Yep!" answered Soppy. "I checked both of them a short while ago. I also made sure all the rest were in order, too. Charlotte, Barnsey, Blankets, Carla and the others... they've each got one. They know what they've got to do as well."

"Excellent!" said Arty. He gave Soppy a wink of approval.

"Right," concluded Brains. "No-one will be wandering around the school. The Entrance Hall and corridor will always be deserted. Once Shanks sees this he'll enter the Head's Office. As soon as he's opened the safe, we'll jump him. Tony has told the Chief Superintendent to storm in at precisely two-forty. Then the game will finally be up for Shanks."

Brains looked round the room. Everyone nodded as they absorbed all the information. It sounded complicated... it was complicated... but it simply had to work. Arty stood up.

"Any questions...?"

"What if Shanks arrives early?"

"He'll have to be stalled. Any more questions?"

Silence.

"No? Excellent! Then let the Fayre begin!"

* * *

Eleven o'clock.

The sweet fragrance of baked cakes and cookies wafted through the warm, April air. Noses twitched whenever anyone caught the smell of them. The odour was indeed divine and one that was most unusual for West Mayling House. Usually, Agnes Brewer's concoctions sent a thick green vapour pouring through the school – causing headaches, stomach aches, a general feeling of nausea and, for some, instant vomiting. What a pleasant change!

The school, of course, was looking its best. The buildings gleamed, sparkled and shone. Once again, West Mayling House stood tall, strong and noble. The grounds looked young, nourished and alive. Lush green leaves adorned the oaks. Beech trees and poplars blossomed. Pathways boasted a spectrum of Spring flowers.

West Mayling – a haven of peace and tranquillity? Not for long!

* * *

Twelve o'clock.

The driveway and the surrounding grounds were packed with vehicles and people heading towards the school buildings. Cars of every description were there, lined up row after row after row. Most were in the expensive category of car – ranging from BMW to Mercedes, from Audi to Volvo and from 4x4 to Rolls Royce and Bentleys. Not a Metro, a Fiat or a Skoda in sight! The people who climbed out of them looked in the expensive category of parent as well.

* * *

One o'clock.

Parents milled around the various stalls. Wellies were being 'wanged' around with gusto. Coconuts were being knocked off their shies. Quiches were being delicately chomped on during the Flan-Eating Contest. It was quite clear, however, which stall was the favourite. Everywhere you looked, parents were eating a cake of some sort, baked by the First Formers. Their food was going down a treat, with parents returning for more – for a second, third or even fourth time during the afternoon.

* * *

One fifty. Precisely.

The PA system now crackled into life. Blankets

McDougal informed the crowd that they should head towards the Hockey Pitch. The Match was about to start...

Parents pricked up their ears. Eyebrows rose. This was something they were definitely looking forward to. The students manning the 'action' stalls started shutting them down – a trick aimed at persuading parents to head promptly for the Hockey Pitch.

Charlotte O'Driscoll had directed her First and Second Form teams to gather into small groups. Each group took a certain pathway and ushered the parents along it as quickly as they could. If any parent showed signs of lagging behind or moving less than enthusiastically, the students grabbed hold of their elbows and began to pick up the pace.

"No need to push!" snapped one older parent, as Hortence Flowers and Gemma Hargreaves literally gripped onto her arms and propelled her forward, her feet hardly touching the ground!

* * *

One fifty-five.

Parents were lining both sides of the Hockey Pitch, with some standing at each end behind the goals. Suddenly, the two teams came running out. Well, at least the children did, anyway. They raced on to the pitch receiving a tremendous ovation from their parents. The teachers ambled along reluctantly –

looking tired and cheesed off – receiving only polite applause from the crowd.

The children began to warm up. The teachers, on the other hand, hung around looking rather lost, not knowing exactly where to stand. Cuthbertson, their goalkeeper for the day, could hardly stand up. Once again, Scotland's smoothest brew had tampered with his ability to function normally. He swayed from side to side, unable to focus his vision and propping himself up precariously against the goalpost.

Reynolds, Bannister, Dickie Howard and Wellie started to perform some stretching manoeuvres. These were short-lived, however, because of the twinges, tweaks and cramps that took over their weary bodies. Barbara Alison stood next to The Saint, nervously discussing some private matters.

Fatty Balshaw was the referee. He'd borrowed a black and white striped jersey to make him look the part. He started counting the players on the pitch, when someone caught his attention. He noticed little Lydia Musgrave limbering up next to Mitch. Fatty was rather concerned, so he waved his friend over to chat with him.

"Are you sure little Lydia should be playing, Mitch? She's only a tiny tot."

"Yeah, I know," remarked Mitch, "but she's a good friend of Soppy's... and Soppy promised her a game."

"Well, look after her, won't you? I don't want to see her hurt."

"Don't worry, Fats. I'll look out for her." He looked over towards little Lydia. "Bless!"

Mitch jogged back over to his team and got them to huddle up. He wanted to give one final 'team-talk' before the game started.

"OK, Team! There are a few things Mr Fox wants us to remember. First, don't forget to –"

"Smash 'em!" interrupted Lydia, pounding her fist into her palm.

The others looked shocked by this outburst from such a delicate looking girl. For a second or two, Mitch didn't quite know what to say. He carried on slowly.

"Yes... thank you, Lydia... but, more importantly... we need to make sure that this game lasts *at least* half an hour. First, we must let the teachers score a few early goals. You know... to keep them happy... to give them hope. Then we can –"

"Smash 'em!" urged Lydia.

"– we can start to chip away at their lead. They'll be tired by then, so this should make it easier for us to –"

"Smash 'em!" shouted Lydia yet again.

Mitch looked at the others and then at Lydia. "It makes it easier to *score*... Lydia." He was most perplexed and not to say a little worried by Lydia, too!

"Yeah... *score*... of course!" yelled Lydia, gritting her teeth. "Then don't forget, guys... smash 'em!"

Mitch knew that, with people like Lydia by his side, there was going to be a high number of casualties on the teachers' team. He wouldn't really have minded if the teachers went down like swatted flies. But – orders were orders.

The main reason why the match was taking place was to keep teachers, parents and the rest of the pupils occupied. Brains had to have everyone out of the way so that he, Tony and Arty could prepare the Head's Office for the imminent arrival of Rory Shanks.

It was, therefore, up to Mitch and Fatty to make sure the game lasted the full thirty minutes – long enough to completely exhaust the teachers. That way, they wouldn't have the energy or inclination to interfere with anything else at the Easter Fayre. It was also imperative to keep the parents engrossed until the next spectacular event...

* * *

Two minutes past two.

Fatty had held out blowing the whistle until the very last moment. He wanted to delay the start for as long as possible. But parents knew the game should kick off at precisely two o'clock and a slow hand-clap echoed around the pitch. Fatty looked over at Mitch. Mitch shrugged his shoulders.

"I guess we're going to have to make a start!" he whispered.

Fatty blew his whistle and the game commenced.

Deliberately, Mitch passed the ball straight to

Barbara Alison. He wanted her to score first. The crowd gasped in shock... Mitch McGovern... Team Captain... supreme school athlete... makes a basic error in hockey? Surely not!

Barbara Alison was an accomplished hockey player in her own right. She could easily have scored a number of goals just by playing her normal game. Even so, she was delighted at being presented this early opportunity and she belted the ball into the back of the net.

One – nil.

The crowd groaned.

Cuthbertson belched.

Craig Jacobs took the re-start ball and masterfully slotted it through Bannister's legs to Rachel O'Hara who was standing in front of the teachers' goal. She lifted her stick, ready to whack the ball home, when she caught sight of Mitch out of the corner of her eye. Mitch very slyly shook his head. It was a sign – *don't* score. In a split-second, Rachel altered her aim and smashed the ball into the left-hand goalpost.

No goal.

The crowd groaned.

Cuthbertson belched.

Mitch winked at Rachel. She understood. Craig realised, too. Mitch really *did* want the teachers to stay in the lead. For how long, though? Surely he wasn't going to let the teachers win?

The game continued.

Dickie Howard tried to swat the ball hard, missed by a mile and fell in a heap on the floor. The parents erupted with applause and laughter. Wellie bumbled up the touchline and called for the ball to be passed his way. Barbara Alison obliged, but Wellie's eyesight wasn't up to scratch. He swiped at it rashly, again missed by a mile and hit himself in the face with his stick. He, too fell in a bundle on the floor.

"Blimey!" tutted Mitch. "They *are* going down like flies! At this rate, the game will be over in ten minutes!"

To top it all, there was one other thing that was worrying him, little Lydia Musgrave. Obviously, Mitch's orders had gone in one ear and straight out the other. She was intent on humiliating the teachers. It was 'win at all costs' for her!

She'd survey the scene very carefully, calculating where Fatty and the crowd were looking. If their attention was elsewhere, she'd prod her hockey stick into a teacher's backside, or 'accidentally' step on their toes. Mitch witnessed these actions on at least a dozen occasions. He whistled to Fatty.

"We've got to keep an eye on her, Fats! We can't let her mow them all down before the thirty minutes are up! That would be disastrous!"

"Agreed."

However, two minutes before half-time, the worst thing happened – Barbara Alison made the mistake of hitting one of Lydia's legs.

Lydia sought revenge – and how!

She ran around, shadowing the PE Teacher for a minute. Then she saw her chance. Alison stopped right next to the advertising boards, waiting for the half-time whistle. The ball trundled to a halt right next to Alison's feet. Lydia weighed up the situation. She looked at Alison, stuck her head down, then charged.

Looking as though she was going for the ball, Lydia pretended to trip. She bent down and stuck her shoulder into the base of the teacher's back. The jolt sent Alison hurtling over the boards. She hit the ground on the other side with an almighty thud and had the wind thoroughly knocked out of her.

Fatty blew his whistle and ran up to Lydia.

"What happened here?" he asked, although he was pretty sure he knew.

"What?" came the innocent reply.

"With Barbara Alison?"

"Who?"

"The PE Teacher."

"Where?"

"Lying on her back down there!"

"How?"

"You tell me!"

"I don't know!" Lydia shrugged her shoulders at Fatty and smiled sweetly at the other teachers. What an angel!

Mitch slapped his hands across his eyes. She'd definitely need a half-time 'talking-to'!

* * *

Brains had rigged up four TV monitors on Devinia's desk. Three were linked to webcams dotted around the grounds – The Hockey Pitch, The Main Hall and the Main Gates. The fourth was for the CCTV cameras positioned above the doors in the Office. He and Arty were busying themselves bolting a camera to the corner of the door frame. Big Tony was standing, half watching the monitors, half looking out of the window.

Suddenly, something caught his eye.

He walked closer to the monitor and squinted hard. He saw a black Mercedes pull slowly through the Main Gates. He raced to the window and peered through his binoculars. The Merc came to a halt on the end of a row of parked cars. The back door opened and a man stepped out...

"Blimey!" he whispered forcefully. "It's Shanks!"

Arty and Brains stopped immediately. "What?"

"Shanks has arrived!"

"Shanks? But we're not ready, yet!"

* * *

Soppy and Sid were rushing about in the Main Hall, preparing things backstage for Godfrey's epic ballet performance.

"Has everything been fixed for the stage, Sid?" Soppy asked.

"Absolutely! Some blocks will creak, others will wobble. Who knows, some may buckle altogether!" Sid sniggered. "Can't wait for this one! Soppy, where's Godfrey?"

"*Where's Godfrey?* You tell me, Sid. I thought *you'd* got him ready for the performance?"

"No," huffed Sid. "It wasn't *my* job to sort Godfrey out. It was yours. Or Barnsey's. It's typical. I'm always asked to do more than my share of the load. It's just not fair."

"Never mind, never mind," tutted Soppy. "*I'll* get him. I just hope he hasn't wandered off towards his Office. If he sees Arty and the others – or Shanks – it'll blow everything. Where did you see him last?"

"I don't know! Soppy, how am I supposed to know something when it wasn't my job in the first place? I'm always asked to do stuff that's not my job!"

"Oh, for goodness sake... moan, moan, moan!"

* * *

Brains and Arty scrambled over to the window. Arty picked up a pair of binoculars and scanned along the driveway.

"Where is he, Tony?"

"Over there... third row along... next to that black Mercedes."

"But that's a blonde-haired man," said Brains.

"He's in disguise!"

243

"Are you *sure* that's him, Tony?"

"Yes, that's him alright!"

"Oh, yes! I can see him now," gasped Arty. "Wow! That's a good disguise! If I hadn't stood so close to him the other night, I would never have recognised him!"

Indeed it was Shanks. He was wearing a false blonde wig and a false beard. Both were very lifelike. The only give-away had been his hooked nose... and that smile.

It was the sort of smile you didn't forget in a hurry. Big Tony and Arty had certainly not forgotten it. The thing that particularly stood out in Arty's memory had been Shanks' gold fillings. Arty remembered how hollow his smile had looked. How it had failed to hide the menace which lay behind his face. Now Arty was looking at a blonde-haired and bearded gentleman, who carried that same look. He knew it could only be one person... Rory Shanks.

Arty radioed through to Soppy.

"He's here! The eagle has landed! Is everything set, Sops?"

* * *

Backstage, Soppy and Sid were still scurrying around, trying to make sure everything was going to plan. One thing was not yet in order, though.

They still couldn't find Godfrey.

Soppy knew that it had definitely been Sid's job to

get him ready *and* keep an eye on him. Sid was sure that he had delegated that responsibility to someone else... but he couldn't quite remember who.

"Sid, you're not half a dozy Muppet!"

"Godfrey's the Muppet! Not me!" huffed Sid. "Arty said so... right at the start of the revolt!"

"Never mind!" tutted Soppy. "Never mind!"

At last she replied to Arty. "Arty... No! We've got trouble over here! Godfrey is on the prowl. He could be coming your way."

"*Our* way! What do you mean – *our way* – Sops? I thought Sid had it all under control?"

"Has he ever?"

"Hmmm. You've got a point there."

"Just be on your guard, Arty. This is critical to the whole success of the operation. Godfrey *must not* see Shanks!"

* * *

"He's got to be stalled!" concluded Brains. "We're simply not ready! We must have the CCTV up and working before he enters here!"

"I've got it!" yelled Arty. He picked up his walkie-talkie and radioed Charlotte. He instructed her to grab half a dozen of the smallest, sweetest, most innocent looking First Form girls as possible. Why? He needed them to divert Shanks' attention. Arty explained the rest of his plan to Charlotte.

* * *

Charlotte managed to round up six girls. Pig-tails, braces, adorable smiles, puppy-eyes throughout – butter wouldn't have melted in their mouths! Charlotte then proceeded to follow Arty's orders to the letter...

Shanks and his two heavies had climbed out of their car, studied the grounds and were about to descend upon the Main Building. Suddenly, the group of schoolgirls came charging towards them.

"What the..." cried Shanks, as two tiny First Formers grabbed hold of his arms.

"Ah, welcome, sir!" announced Charlotte. "We saw you standing here, looking a little lost. We thought to ourselves: 'They must be new to the school.' So it's our duty and pleasure to give you... a guided tour!"

"A bloomin' what?" gasped Shanks.

"Oh! It's the very least we can do!" interrupted Charlotte. "Now, come on girls! Forward march!"

Without hesitating, Charlotte pointed her arm straight ahead and strode off. The six other girls paired up – two on each man – and gripped on for dear life. Sweetly smiling at Shanks and the heavies, they surged forward, dragging the hapless trio towards the cake stall... and away from the Main Building.

* * *

"She's a star – that Charlotte O'Driscoll," smiled Arty, as he watched through his binoculars.

He picked up the walkie-talkie. "Charlie, you're doing fabulously! Keep it going for as long as you can. If it helps, I reckon Mr Shanks and his 'intellectuals' would love a mountain of flapjacks, a close look at the Spring flowers in the school gardens, followed by a good ten minute chat on the Second Form needlework display in the Art Block!"

Charlotte heard every word and nodded her head. Big Tony – looking through his binoculars – saw her gesture and informed Arty that she'd understood.

"Excellent!" sighed Arty. "At least – now – things will go smoothly..."

"Blast!" snapped Brains.

"What is it, Brains?" gasped Arty, swivelling round quickly and staring at his friend.

"I don't believe it! I've gone and fused the CCTV camera!"

* * *

The crowd clapped and cheered as both teams sat down for a well-earned half-time rest. Three parents took trays of drinks over to the children. Refreshing, ice-cool, freshly-squeezed lemon juice with mint, cane sugar and ice cubes, followed by Lucozade Sport and slices of juicy Seville oranges. The teachers were taken steaming mugs of milky hot chocolate and double-chocolate muffins with whipped cream.

Mitch noticed the distinct difference in healthiness of the snack that had been arranged for each team. A thought came to him and he grabbed Fatty Balshaw.

"Fats – swap the drinks!"

"You what?"

"Swap the refreshments over!"

"Why?"

"Think about it. We need to keep this game going for another fifteen minutes or so."

"And?"

"Well, just look at the teachers! They're cream-crackered! They're on their last knees! They'll never survive! What's more... look at their half-time snack!"

Fatty looked over at the calorie-filled trays. "I still don't see what you're getting at, Mitch."

"If they eat all that... and we consume this stuff... they'll be full up and lethargic... we'll be buzzing and alert."

"So?"

"So... it should be the other way round! They need the energy! And to be quite frank, little Lydia could do with slowing down!"

Fatty suddenly understood. What a great idea! He winked at Mitch, then raced over to the parents. He smiled, grabbed the teachers' trays and returned them to Mitch and his team. He then picked up the students' stimulating refreshments and took them over to the bedraggled teachers.

They looked particularly puzzled but they guzzled down the energy-bursting beverages in record time. As Mitch hoped, a sparkle was returning to their faces.

Mitch, on the other hand, started to hand over the stodgy double-chocolate muffins to Lydia.

"There you go, Lydia, get stuck in! This is terrific food for energy, you know!"

"That's right," added Craig. "Go on, Lydia, make a pig of yourself!"

"Yeah!" chuckled the rest of the team. "Take your shoes and socks off, and dive in!"

So she did...

* * *

Lydia wasn't the only one stuffing her face. Rory Shanks was being supplied with endless goodies, too. Charlotte made him and the heavies taste every home-made patisserie on offer at the Easter Fayre. A flapjack, two iced buns, a custard Danish, one mince pie, two rock cakes, a chocolate 'crispie', one slice of jam sponge, two slices of toffee cheesecake... and a cream doughnut. All consumed within five minutes.

Arty's plan was working a treat. Shanks didn't have the nerve to argue with or offend such sweet and innocent young girls. He may have posted his enemies to their Grandmothers through the mail... but he felt very uneasy being bossed around by eleven-year-old girls!

Hardball Rory Shanks was contained, for now...

* * *

Brains was working away in the Head's Office. He'd tried to add too many appliances to one electrical socket and had blown the camera fuse. Brains was annoyed to say the very least.

"Who would have guessed that this one socket – the very one that I decide to choose – is probably the oldest in West Mayling! I can't believe it. Of all the luck!"

"How long will it take to fix, Brains?" asked Arty.

"A few minutes, I guess!"

Arty turned to Big Tony. "Any sign of Shanks?"

"Not yet," replied Big Tony, "but I see that the second half of the Hockey Match has just begun..."

* * *

Backstage. Soppy and Sid were still hunting for the Headmaster.

"Was that the whistle I just heard, Sid?"

They looked at each other in desperation.

"The second half," gulped Sid.

"Right. Fifteen minutes, Sid, and they'll all be here! We've got to find Godfrey – now!"

* * *

Fatty had blown his whistle hard.

Once again, he'd attempted to stall for time. He'd stretched out the half-time break for as long as possible but, again, the parents were on the ball. They knew when the second half should have started and another slow hand-clap had begun. Fatty knew that he couldn't risk any of them departing and wandering around the school. So he signalled to Mitch and waved play to begin.

Miraculously, the teachers looked fairly perky – the refreshments must have worked. Barbara Alison had virtually recovered from Lydia's bashing and was bouncing up and down on her feet, eager for more action. Even Dickie and old Wellie looked sprightly.

The students picked themselves up. Lydia let out a rasping burp... and patted her stomach. Full to the brim! Mitch glanced at her.

"Excellent!" he thought. "That should calm her down a bit!"

The crowd started chanting from the sides of the pitch. They wanted their team to play a little better this half. However, following orders again, Mitch let the first ball glide under his stick and straight into the path of Bannister.

The crowd gasped.

Another error from the Captain!

Bannister dribbled the ball up field and did quite a good job of it, too. He swerved it past a few children, retained possession of it brilliantly... then shot. Rachel

O'Hara, goalkeeper for the second half, deliberately let it past.

Goal.

Two – nil.

The crowd groaned.

Cuthbertson belched once again.

Despite feeling heat from the parents' eyes, Mitch stuck to his plan. He ordered his team to let in one more goal. They did. The teachers were elated and they suddenly became determined to defend this winning lead.

Mitch had taken a calculated gamble with the parents. Yes, they could have walked away in disgust... but he guessed otherwise. He reckoned they'd want to stay and watch the drama unfold. Could the students return from three – nil down?

With just three minutes left on the clock, he huddled together with his team.

"Right. First, well done to all you guys! I know it's not easy letting the teachers gain the upper hand. But it had to be done."

"What does that mean?" asked Lydia, burping.

"Never mind, Lydia, never mind! Just concentrate now on winning! That goes for the rest of you. We've done our job. We've kept everyone here for the right amount of time. Now it's our turn to have some fun."

"Does that mean we can... smash 'em?" asked Lydia.

"*Yes*, Lydia! *Now* we can... 'smash 'em'!"

Mitch took the bully off, passing the ball to Craig. Immediately Bannister crashed into them and stole the ball. He charged up field towards Rachel O'Hara, fully intent on scoring again.

Mitch wasn't going to let *that* happen! He stuck to Bannister closely – just one step behind. Bannister twisted suddenly to his left and headed for the goal. He was only two metres away. Mitch looked up and smiled. He knew exactly what to do – and timed his shove to perfection...

Mitch's crafty nudge sent Bannister toppling completely off balance. More tripping over than running gracefully, Bannister crashed straight into the hollow goal posts. He fell over backwards – dazed, confused, completely out of it.

The crowd breathed in sharply.

Cuthbertson belched – very loudly.

The parents sympathised with Bannister's grave misfortune – but not for very long. They soon turned their attention back to the game and the PE Teacher's groaning and grumbling was ignored again. Poor old Bannister, it just wasn't his term!

Mind you, this term wasn't any kinder to The Bear, either.

His game ended prematurely in a right royal style.

He'd managed to acquire the hockey ball and had knocked it straight down the middle of the park. Dusty Clive Shaw and The Saint were standing on opposite flanks of the pitch. They saw Reynolds whack the ball and both charged after it. Reynolds chased after it, too – staying just a metre behind.

The ball arrived on the centre spot.

So did all three teachers.

Heads down, eyes fixed on the ball, oblivious to where anyone else was, The Saint and Dusty Shaw sandwiched Reynolds between them in one *almighty* wallop! The three bodies bounced off each other and The Bear withered to the ground like a leaf falling from a tree.

* * *

Big Tony saw the collision on the webcam monitor. "Ouch!" he chuckled. "I bet that hurt!"

* * *

Mitch took possession of the ball. He scurried past Barbara Alison, who was far too concerned with The Saint's condition to be thinking about the Match, and slammed the ball past Cuthbertson.

Three – One.

The crowd yelled with glee.

Cuthbertson carried on belching.

Two minutes to go. Three goals needed for a win.

Dickie Howard did his level best to hold on to the ball, but Lydia easily out-muscled him. She shoved him out of the way and dribbled the ball down the right-hand side. Looking ahead, she passed the ball directly to Becky DeMont, who walloped it past the Science Teacher.

Three – Two.

The crowd cheered.

Cuthbertson belched horribly.

The final minute. At the re-start: virtually the same scenario. Lydia thoroughly embarrassed Dickie by knocking him off the ball. She then dribbled the ball forward – this time, taking it all the way herself. She looked up, shot and scored.

Three – Three.

The crowd erupted.

Cuthbertson belched yet again and finally flopped down. Scotch whisky, a long fizzy drink and too much excitement had taken their toll. He could no longer prop himself up. His legs gave way and he came crashing to the floor. Mitch looked on and smiled.

Then he stopped and thought.

Cuthbertson was such a huge mound of flesh that his body covered virtually the entire goal-mouth. With less than a minute to go, they still needed one more goal. How would they score past that lump?

He made up his mind. It would be up to him – Mitch McGovern... star player... Team Captain... and student with a reputation to rebuild amongst parents – to save the day.

Craig tackled Dickie Howard straight from the re-start. How embarrassing – three times in as many minutes Dickie had lost the ball to the opposition! Craig passed it to Mitch and Mitch headed for goal.

He dribbled the ball easily around a totally deflated Philipe Saint-Moreaux, ran it past an equally dejected Sebastian Bannister and cleverly knocked it through the legs of a bruised Clive Shaw. With just five metres to go, Mitch slowed right down. Head up, he took aim. He carefully angled the head of his stick then delicately chipped the ball over Cuthbertson's snoozing body. The ball plopped into the back of the net.

Four – Three to the students.

The crowd roared and cheered.

Mitch was a hero once more!

Fatty blew his whistle to signal the game was over.

Victory, again, to the students!

* * *

"Yesss!" yelled Big Tony as he watched the goal on the webcam monitor.

Arty checked his watch. Two-thirty.

The final countdown had begun...

* * *

Up to this point, Charlotte's team was still firmly in control of Rory Shanks. They'd dragged him and the heavies over to the Spring flowers and had bored them to death with a chat on how the ground staff had managed such a beautiful display.

However, on the way to the Art Block to see the fascinating needlework mural, disaster struck... The students had just scored the fourth and final goal, and the crowd had exploded. The six girls were startled by the tremendous noise and let loose their grip on the gangsters.

Charlotte noticed that Shanks had now become free. He straightened his tie, adjusted his waistcoat and cleared his throat.

"Touched as I am with this... riveting tour... I 'ave urgent business elsewhere. So... ladies... if you don't mind."

Shanks clicked his fingers. The two heavies turned immediately and followed their boss. The three men started to head back towards the Main Building.

* * *

Two thirty-two.

Next on the entertainment agenda for parents was the ballet performance in the Main Hall. Billed as having a 'Guest Ballerina' on all the latest flyers, it had generated a great deal of interest amongst the intrigued parents. Tony watched them again from Devinia's Office through his binoculars.

"OK, guys, the parents are on their way to the Main Hall."

"All of them?" enquired Brains.

"Er... no... actually..."

"What do you mean... *no?*" interrupted Brains.

"It looks as if there's a couple of old crumblies heading this way!"

"That's no good!" snapped Brains. "They've *all* got to go straight into the Hall. We said that right from the start!"

"Tony," interrupted Arty, "can you see anyone who can sort this?"

Big Tony scanned the grounds. He saw Charlotte O'Driscoll racing along one of the pathways towards the Main Building.

"Yes – Charlotte."

"Charlotte? What – with Shanks?"

"No – on her own."

"*On her own?* Blimey! Right... well... radio her. Ask her where Shanks is. And tell her to grab the grannies. She'll have to escort them away."

Big Tony picked up the walkie-talkie. He relayed Arty's demands to Charlotte. She frantically waved her arms – indicating to them that Shanks was now on the loose.

Tony signalled back that he'd got the message, then pointed to the old ladies on her right.

Even though Charlotte wanted desperately to catch up with Shanks, she realised she'd have to alter her plans. The two old ladies had to be stopped. She scampered up to them, hooked her hands under their

258

armpits, and quickly marched them in the opposite direction.

"*All sorted*," Tony stated, "thanks to Charlotte." He turned to Arty. "Right, do you want the good news or the bad?"

"Meaning?"

"Well, the good news is that the grannies are no longer a problem."

"And the bad?"

"There's no sign of the Police yet and Shanks has escaped. He could be anywhere."

"Perfect," sighed Arty. "So... *not* all sorted, eh, Tony!"

* * *

Two thirty-three.

The Main Hall filled rapidly, with hum-drum chatter and idle conversation echoing through the air. The School Orchestra was warming up in front of the stage, still sounding more like a cat screeching from a treetop than a swan gracefully gliding across a lake...

* * *

Two thirty-four.

Hortence Flowers and Gemma Hargreaves were ushering the remaining stragglers into the Hall. The grounds at last were empty. The only people moving were the teachers, on their way to the Pavilion – as ordered – to take their showers.

However, no-one had seen Rory Shanks now for four whole minutes. He was on the loose and hungry for money...

* * *

Two thirty-five.

The lights flickered on and off. The music began, much more sweetly than the practice had promised! The stage curtains parted and the background scenery – painted by Pablo Durrant – received a deserved accolade of applause. Tension mounted, as the parents waited patiently for the 'Guest Ballerina' to make 'her' entrance...

* * *

Mitch joined the three other boys in Devinia's Office. They were waiting for the real entertainment of the day to start: the capture of Rory Shanks. This couldn't take place until the CCTV was repaired and Brains was still furiously working away on it. Arty was assisting with whatever he could. Every now and again he'd pop his head up and look at the webcam monitors.

He could see the deserted Hockey Pitch and could just make out the teachers entering the Pavilion on their way to shower and change. Finally, he could see the Main Hall – now packed full to the rafters.

Big Tony suddenly whistled.

"I've just spotted Shanks! He's heading our way! We're on!"

Tony saw the gangster boss strolling around some of the empty stalls. He was scanning the grounds to make doubly sure no-one was following him. Arty looked at Brains attempting to fix the damaged plug.

"What do you reckon?"

"Not quite, Arty. Nearly there... but not quite."

"OK... I don't want to panic you, my friend, but the whole capture rests upon you fixing that."

"So, no pressure then, eh, Arty?" scoffed Brains.

"No, not really. It's just that you've probably got... oh, I would say about... two minutes... that's all."

* * *

Two thirty-seven.

The orchestra carried on playing and the audience patiently waited. But as the music continued on and on... the crowd's excitement changed into curiosity. After the fourth minute of music, their curiosity turned to disappointment. The crowd began to get restless.

Soppy's stress levels were at bursting point. Where the dickens was Godfrey? She'd hunted everywhere – high and low – but still no sign of him. She radioed Arty and told him the situation.

Arty slapped his hands across his eyes. Could any more things go wrong today?

Both he and Soppy thought quickly and came up with a plan...

Fearing some of the parents would get up and walk out, Soppy grabbed hold of Barnsey.

"We've got to play for time," she said.

"Meaning what?" replied Barnsey.

"Meaning... you've got to go on stage and make an announcement."

"An announcement? Me?"

"Yes."

"About what?"

"Well, tell them there's going to be a... meeting... after the ballet... outside the Pavilion... at three o'clock."

"What was all that?" asked Barnsey. But too late! Soppy shoved him firmly and he stumbled out on to centre stage.

Barnsey was nervous. He glanced at all the eyes. There were hundreds, all staring at him. He waved at the Orchestra to stop them playing. Eventually, when they halted, Barnsey gulped and cleared his throat.

"Er... There's going to be a crass beating at two o'clock..."

"*A mass meeting!*" hissed Soppy from the side of the stage. "At *three*... you silly..."

"Er... I mean... a mass meeting at three o'clock," croaked Barnsey. "In the Pub –"

262

"The *Pavilion*... you stupid..." hissed Soppy again, holding her forehead.

"Er... in the Pavilion... at three... tomorrow... er... I mean, today!"

It was no good. Soppy couldn't wait any longer. She stormed out on to the stage and faced the audience. In her best British accent, she delivered her speech to the crowd.

"Ladies and Gentlemen, I do apologise for the slight delay to proceedings. I would like to announce – before the exquisite ballet performance begins – that Mr Godfrey Randolph Mannering would like to invite you all to an impromptu meeting, today, at three o'clock, outside the Pavilion. He has some terribly important news to tell you. So, until later..."

Soppy bowed and nodded to the audience. Then, quite unceremoniously, she grabbed Barnsey by his ear and dragged him off-stage. Parents raised the odd eyebrow – talk about 'girl-power'!

To the side of the stage, Soppy turned and faced Barnsey.

"If you want something done properly... you've got to do it yourself. Isn't that right... *Alex?*"

* * *

Mitch wandered out of Devinia's Office, across the Entrance Hall and up the staircase. He peered out of the window. Still no sign of the Police...

* * *

Big Tony was scanning the grounds through his binoculars. Arty was pacing up and down the Head's Office. He looked at his watch and then at Brains.

"I'd say... about sixty seconds now..."

* * *

The School Orchestra continued playing.

Out of the blue, Soppy found the Head. He was backstage, sitting on a chair, reading a newspaper. Soppy shook her head. How had she missed him sitting there? Where on earth had he been? Whatever, she breathed a sigh of relief and whistled for Sid to join her. Sid approached the Head forthrightly.

"Come on Godfrey, get your finger out!"

"I want none of your lip, Gumbar!" bellowed the Head, folding his arms.

"Really?" Sid smiled. "Well, can I remind you who out of the two of us is wearing a pink tutu? Do you really think I'm going to listen to you?"

"Damned cheek!" griped the Head.

"Now, now, Godfrey! Mind your language in front of the ladies!"

"Poppycock! To think that I, Godfrey Randolph Mannering, am standing here – in a pink tutu – having to put up with this nonsense from you, Gumbar." The Head raised his eyebrows. "In fact, I *don't* have to put up with this, do I? I've changed my mind... I'm not going to do it, after all!"

"You'll do it," Soppy blurted out, "or you'll go to jail, Godfrey!"

"You haven't got the nerve, young lady!"

"Really? Watch me!" Soppy took a firm grip of the Head and shoved him towards the stage. "Now get out there!"

"No! I won't do it! You can't make me!"

"Oh yes, we bloomin' well can!" grunted Soppy, pushing with all her might. "Out! You lazy lump!"

One more sturdy shove from Soppy propelled the Head onto centre stage. The crowd sat totally stunned. Their jaws dropped, their eyes glazed, they stared in disbelief. For in front of them was a sight they never imagined they'd witness. It was their esteemed Headmaster, Godfrey Randolph Mannering, standing in a swan's pose. He was dressed in a pink tutu and pink, silk ballet shoes, but was *still* wearing his mortarboard!

Intensifying the moment of drama, the Orchestra stopped playing once again.

Silence reigned throughout the Hall.

Godfrey wobbled on one leg. He was trying hard to maintain his balance in his swan's pose. At first, the Headmaster ignored the silence but he couldn't ignore the temptation to look at the crowd for long. His eyes began wandering around the Hall...

He saw the shocked expressions on the parents'

faces. He saw Paul Pablo Durrant, the Art Teacher, sitting in the front row. Pablo picked up his charcoals and began sketching the Headmaster.

Godfrey closed his eyes and shook his head. He asked himself why he'd done it. He wondered if it *was* actually worth the money. He then pictured what the result would be and cringed at the thought that people would never let him live this down.

* * *

Two thirty-eight.

Shanks paused before making his move. He wandered over towards the Main Building. The two heavies followed, but at a distance behind him. Tony saw them approaching. Brains had just taped up the last cable to the CCTV camera and flicked the switch. He held his breath. The red light appeared. It was working!

Arty and Brains grabbed two monitors each and hid them behind Devinia's desk. They then crouched behind these, out of sight to anyone inside Devinia's Office. Tony left the room and took up his position in Godfrey's Office.

"Is the *bird* in the *cage*, Sops?" whispered Arty into his walkie-talkie. He desperately wanted to know where Godfrey was.

"Oh, yes!" came the chuckling reply. "The bird has been found, tethered and thrown onto centre stage.

You should see him – he looks lovely in pink!"

Arty smiled. "Understood, Sops. Over and out!" He breathed deeply.

Relief. Now their fun would really begin...

* * *

Two-thirty-nine.

Shanks now checked out the Main Building. He pretended to admire the school photographs on the Entrance Hall walls. All the while, he diverted his eyes to check that the coast was clear.

One heavy remained outside the Front Door. The second wandered inside, past Devinia's Office and the Staffroom, then on a little further. He eventually stopped outside the Kitchen, guarding the corridor that led to the Main Hall. His job was to make sure no-one came out of the ballet performance.

Shanks took one final look around... then swiftly entered Devinia's Office. Immediately he froze...

The Orchestra had suddenly piped up again in the Main Hall. Their noise had startled him – he wasn't expecting anything like that.

* * *

It also woke the audience up and snapped them out of their trance. With their concentration back, they began to laugh at Godfrey.

Soon, everyone realised how ridiculous he looked. The whole audience erupted with howls and cheers, followed by cheeky wolf-whistles as well.

"Lovely legs, Headmaster!" yelled one parent.

"I fancy the bird in pink!" cried another.

Parents roared even louder. Soppy was chuckling backstage, too. Sid took photos of each twirl and jump the Head attempted. "There's one for the Entrance Hall wall!" he said, snapping another picture on his camera. "Sops, are you ready with the flooring?"

"Oh, yes!"

* * *

Nerves were on edge in Devinia's Office. Nothing could be left to chance. Rory Shanks was not a man you crossed and lived to tell the tale. If he was going to be caught, it had to be perfectly timed – right in the middle of him stealing the goods. Arresting him red-handed would allow the Police to win their case in Court. They would then see him go to prison for a goodly number of years.

The concealed CCTV camera followed Shanks' footsteps, as he crept past the desk and entered the Headmaster's Office.

A look of satisfaction spread over the gangster's face. Big Tony's promise that every door would be open was true. Shanks rubbed his hands with glee and smiled.

* * *

Mitch had hidden himself on the First Floor balcony, overlooking the Entrance Hall. He glanced through the small, rectangular window. Still no sign of the Police!

* * *

Studying the Head's every move, Sid and Soppy waited. As soon as he'd approached a target block, they acted. The Head jumped into the air. He tried to twist around a full circle – three-sixty degrees – and land delicately on both feet. Just as he was about to hit the stage, Soppy yanked a rope.

The stage block sunk three inches.

The Head landed – one foot on a higher stage block, the other foot on the lower block. It tipped him completely off balance and he lurched uncontrollably forward. Tripping over his feet, he dived head first into the School Orchestra – bursting through the skin of the huge bass drum. This sent a dull boom around the Hall, throwing the audience and Orchestra into yet more fits of laughter. The Orchestra just about managed to keep playing – not an easy task at all!

The Head got up and wearily climbed back on stage. He danced about a bit more, twisting here and bending low there. He moved to the back of the stage then skipped forward to the front.

Soppy nodded at Sid.

He pulled another rope which was attached to a fake theatre light. Carla O'Driscoll had constructed it out of sugar-glass and tin foil. It wobbled precariously for just a few seconds, then fell directly onto Godfrey Mannering's head.

The sugar-glass cracked easily, but the foil still caused a lovely ripping sound as it made contact with Godfrey. Unbeknown to Sid and Soppy, Carla had also placed six eggs inside the fake light. These cracked upon impact, oozing yolk and albumen slowly down the Headmaster's face.

The crowd howled with laughter and pointed in fits of hysterics. Godfrey wiped the yoke from his eyes and took a long, slow, deep breath. Just a couple more minutes, and a final leap would end this humiliation once and for all...

* * *

Two forty-one.

Shanks had already removed the 17th Century Duke from its hooks. He rested it against the cabinet just as he'd done during the gambling evening. He went through exactly the same procedure as then. He breathed on his fingers, rubbed the tips on his jacket lapel, grabbed hold of the dial on the safe and placed his ear against the door. He turned the dial to the right, to the left, then back to the right. The magic sound of a deeper, heavier 'click' greeted his ears.

He'd cracked the combination again, even though Brains had altered it a week before!

He was now in business.

* * *

Mitch scratched his head. He peered out of the window again and feverishly scanned the grounds...

Still no sign of the Police.

* * *

Two forty-two.

Godfrey was about to perform his finale. He was meant to spring from one side of the stage to the other, resembling an elegant swan in flight. He leapt up high, spreading his legs wide apart. Watching from the side, Sid pulled yet another rope.

But something went wrong this time.

The rope snapped.

The stage block dropped completely to the floor. The Head closed his eyes and landed smack in the centre of the missing block. He crashed out of sight – making a thunderous din – just as the Orchestra reached the last few bars of their music.

A cloud of dust wafted up from the hole in the stage. Rapturous applause followed from the parents, who leapt immediately to their feet. They'd loved it! They'd never been so entertained in their lives!

The audience stood there cheering – and calling for an encore!

* * *

Shanks was just about to pull the handle to the safe when the loud roar erupted in the Main Hall.

The Head had just fallen through the stage.

It was such a *sudden* noise that it startled Shanks again. He stopped and turned around, pressing his body flat against the wall. He listened for a short while, then carried on. He took hold of the handle and smiled. The door was about to open...

* * *

It was such a *loud* noise that it dislodged a small particle of dust in Devinia's Office which fell from a shelf and entered Brain's nose. He felt a strong tickling sensation shoot right through it and pinched his nostrils together. He held his breath and waited. When he thought it had passed, he released the pressure on his nose.

The second he did that, the urge returned and a short, sharp sneeze burst out.

Arty and Big Tony froze. Even though it had made only the very slightest noise, it was enough to send a shiver down their spines.

Shanks, next door, had heard this sound, too. He

let go of the handle, spun round again and pressed his body hard up against the wall. He narrowed his eyebrows. Where had that noise come from?

Nothing stirred.

He returned to the safe for the third time.

* * *

Two forty-three.

Three minutes late, the Police arrived at the Main Gates.

Mitch sighed with relief. Even though he could take care of himself, he knew his limitations – he'd stand no chance against the two heavies. He glanced outside again. The Police looked determined and ready for action...

* * *

Parents in the Main Hall rose to their feet.

Sid and Soppy beamed with pride. They'd done it! They were bang on time! They walked out onto centre stage and – avoiding the hole – held hands, bowed and curtsied.

The parents cheered even louder, still calling for more from Godfrey.

Godfrey was clambering out of the hole, when Sid took a step backwards and trod on his fingers. The Head howled and let go. He immediately fell back under the stage, sending another dust-cloud upwards.

Sid threw kisses out to the audience. He lapped up all the attention and praise. Soppy smiled and shook her head. She loved Sid – even though she knew he was a clown!

* * *

Shanks heard this encore roar coming from the Main Hall and decided to work much faster. He pulled the handle sharply and the safe door opened. He gazed inside and saw what he'd come for... wads and wads of cash.

Shanks didn't waste time gloating on his find. He stuck his hand into his jacket pocket and pulled out a folded cloth bag. He started thrusting the wads of cash deep inside. Working at speed, it still took him a couple of minutes to empty the safe. Once he was finished, he turned to exit the room, leaving the safe door wide open.

Arty, Brains and Big Tony leapt to their feet. There was a sudden, silent but potentially deadly stand-off.

"Not so fast, Mr Shanks!" announced Arty.

"You!" blurted out Shanks in surprise. "What do you want, you 'saft' little waiter-boy?"

"Now that's not very polite, is it, Mr Shanks?"

"You what?"

"Here I am, trying to have a civilised conversation, and you have to spoil it by being coarse and hostile."

"Do you want some free medical advice, boy?" growled Shanks.

"If I must!"

"Shut ya gob and get out me way!"

"Sorry," muttered Arty, rubbing his chin. "No can do, I'm afraid!"

"What?" snapped Shanks. "Get out of it, you idiot! Just remember who you're dealing with here. Now push off before you get hurt. Don't want you running off and crying to ya Mummy, now, do we!"

"I hate to disappoint you, Shanks-me-old-Hearty, but you're not looking at three Lord Fauntleroys here, you know."

"Is that so?"

"Did you *really* think we were going to stand here and let you take a million quid from us, just like that?"

"Shut up, Cupcake! You're beginning to bore me."

"Charming... Baldy!" hissed Arty.

"Watch it... Softy!" replied Shanks.

"Punk!"

"Well, *I* hate to cut short this luvly chat," sniffed Shanks, "but as Biggles once said... 'I must fly'!"

Shanks bent down to pick up his sack. Big Tony spun round, grabbed a decanter of whisky and aimed it straight at Shanks.

"Fancy a drop of scotch, Shanks?"

He lobbed the bottle at the gangster boss. It missed – and smashed on the wall behind him. Arty looked at Tony.

"A shameful waste of some damn fine booze!"

"Arty!" tutted Brains. "Get a grip!"

Arty shrugged. "OK!" He picked up another glass decanter – full of brandy – and hurled this one at Shanks as well. Again, it flew over his head and smashed against the wall. The noise of shattering glass, however, alerted the heavies – and also the Police outside.

* * *

Two forty-five.

The two heavies came rushing from their positions into the corridor. Mitch whistled from the top of the stairs to attract their attention. He was holding the largest trophy the school had – the Champion House Winners' Cup.

It was huge – three feet in height and made of solid silver. It had two large handles and looked like a giant FA Cup. Mitch had bolted a pulley system to the ceiling. He'd threaded a rope through it and had attached the end to one of the handles.

Mitch let go of the trophy.

It swung down low and fast, catching one of the heavies clean in the stomach.

One down.

One to go!

The second heavy looked on in astonishment. Instead of racing into the Headmaster's Office to help his boss, he turned his aggression towards Mitch. He started to climb the staircase. Mitch swallowed hard. This would be a test of his strength and power!

At that moment, three hefty policemen at last burst through the huge Front Door. They immediately chased the heavy and jumped on his back. A short scuffle ensued, but the heavy didn't stand much chance. He soon found himself in handcuffs.

* * *

Back inside the Headmaster's Office, Shanks was still on the loose... and still very dangerous.

Tony picked up the last decanter of brandy and attempted a third strike. Shanks ducked yet again and the decanter sailed past him, straight into the safe – spraying liquid and broken glass deep inside the wall.

Now the boys had no more objects to throw. Shanks leered at them and set off confidently for the door. Big Tony quickly dived into Shanks' shins, managing to trip him up. Shanks fell backwards, dropped the sack and most of the cash spilled out over the floor.

Arty looked desperately round the room. He noticed the large framed portrait of the Headmaster, hanging on the wall next to him. It was set behind a very thick piece of glass. Arty rushed over to it, scanned the frame and raised an eyebrow. He reckoned it would weigh quite a bit!

He glanced back at Shanks – who'd jumped to his feet and was stuffing the money back into his sack. Big Tony was just picking himself up, completely winded after his hefty tackle.

Shanks looked flustered – as he hastily grasped the last wads of cash.

Arty knew time was running out. He climbed up onto the drinks cabinet next to Godfrey's portrait and reached up to unhook it. He whipped out his penknife and cut loose the string that attached it to hooks on the wall.

"Timber!" shouted Arty.

He watched the huge heavy picture arc away from the wall. Brains turned round immediately. Big Tony coughed and looked upwards. Shanks stopped for a split-second... then gulped.

The frame came crashing down – right over the gangster's head. The glass cracked and the canvas tore. Shanks groaned and fell flat on the floor once again. Brains studied the wreckage – then looked down at Tony. Tony winked – he would live! He glanced at Arty.

"That's right, girls!" grinned Arty, looking at Godfrey's ruined portrait. "Rory Shanks... framed for attempted robbery!"

The Master had been felled!

West Mayling was no longer the Servant!

Chapter 19

Calm Waters

Two fifty-five.

Calm waters had returned to West Mayling House.

At the end of the ballet performance, the parents began filtering out of the Main Hall and were heading towards the Pavilion. Charlotte's teams of First and Second Formers were, once again, shepherding them in the right direction. Despite this, the parents still managed to catch a glimpse of the Main Building.

They looked as stunned by this scene as they had been on seeing the Headmaster in a pink tutu. The Police had swooped into the school and had sealed off the Main Gates and drive. Officers were swarming all around, blue lights were flashing as far as the eye could see and the sound of voices speaking through walkie-talkies echoed everywhere.

A police van was parked close to the Main Building with its back doors wide open. Inside sat the two heavies, handcuffed, subdued and looking very solemn indeed. The Detective Chief Superintendent was inside Devinia's Office, talking with Arty and the others. Suddenly, a dust-covered and beaten-looking

Godfrey Mannering wobbled inside the doorway.

"What the hell's going on here?" he spluttered. "Why are all these Police around the school, Fox?"

"Ah, you must be Godfrey Mannering, Headmaster of West Mayling House," interrupted the Chief Superintendent. He looked at the state of the Head and furrowed his brow. "Good grief, man," he mocked, "what have you been doing? What on earth are you wearing? Is that a tutu?"

Arty and the others smiled.

"I have been doing a spot of ballet, Officer," mumbled Mannering wearily. Then, remembering his position – as the tone of the Chief's voice hit home – he perked up a little. "In my profession, Officer, one has to get involved with children's work! We teachers aren't afraid to join in, you know! It's all in the good name of education!"

"Yes, well, rather you than me, Mr Mannering. That's all I have to say on that subject!"

* * *

Three o'clock.

Following the arrest of Rory Shanks, the Chief Superintendent told Arty they *would* get a reward for their bravery. Arty was delighted – more money for the school – and persuaded him to join them down at the Pavilion. Once the other Police Officers had escorted the gangster boss and his colleagues away, the Chief strolled along to hear what the meeting was all about.

The crowd was buzzing with curiosity as Arty climbed the Pavilion steps. He gazed at the gathering of parents, teachers and students standing near the Hockey Pitch. They were all facing him... wondering what the important news was going to be.

"Ladies and Gentlemen... boys and girls... I'm sure you will agree that this year's Easter Fayre has been a rip-roaring success!"

The parents cheered and whooped.

"But... before we bring the day's events to a close, we have one *final* announcement to make..."

The audience clapped in expectation.

"Before further ado, let me introduce to you... creator of the modern, state-of-the-art West Mayling House... Shepherd to his Flock... and good all round sport... your Headmaster, Godfrey Randolph Mannering!"

Arty held out his arm. Sid and Mitch grabbed hold of Godfrey and led him up the steps.

The Head was greeted with even more enthusiastic applause.

Godfrey, however, bemused and still covered in dust, looked somewhat annoyed.

"What the blazes are you playing at, Fox!" he boomed. "What is all this nonsense? Why did I see Shanks outside my Office in that police van?"

Chief Superintendent Benjamin raised an eyebrow.

Had he heard the Headmaster correctly? If so, how did *he* know Rory Shanks?

Arty placed his hand over the microphone and glared into Mannering's eyes.

"If you blow the game this late in the day... you're a fool," he said quietly.

"What are you rabitting on about, Fox?"

"Keep it zipped and just... go with the flow..."

"Go with the flow..?"

"Yes! If you want to keep that backside of yours out of jail –"

"Damned cheek!"

"– just follow my lead..."

Arty took his hand away from the microphone. He turned, faced the crowd and smiled.

"Ladies and gentlemen, the big news of the day is... I'm very sorry to say... Godfrey Mannering is leaving West Mayling House..."

The crowd were stunned into silence.

"Leaving?" whimpered Godfrey.

"Yes, Mr Mannering has decided to resign..."

The crowd let out gasps of shock.

"Resign?" he whispered. "Right now? *This* term?"

"Yes, Headmaster!" hissed Arty. "You *have* already resigned! Remember our little agreement?"

He turned to look at the audience. "It's such a great pity... for us all."

"A *great* pity," echoed Sid, standing behind Arty.

"We were all mortally upset by the announcement

282

Mr Mannering made in Assembly – *yesterday*."

"*Mortally*," repeated Sid.

"Announcement?" queried the Head, confused and dazed. "Assembly? Yesterday? I don't recall..."

Arty interrupted by feigning a loud laugh. He put his hand on the microphone once again and spoke to Godfrey through gritted teeth.

"If you want that hundred and twenty-five grand... keep your trap shut!"

"What? Hey?" spluttered the Head. "I don't need your blessed money, boy! I'm more than comfortably off, thank you very much. So I'll retire when I like –"

"We know all about that million in your safe!" Arty cut in.

Silence! Horror!

"And it ain't going into your pocket, *Godfrey*... that's for sure!"

Godfrey's jaw dropped.

"It's going straight back into *our* school... where it belongs!"

"That's unless you want to explain it to the Chief Superintendent here," added Soppy.

More silence.

Godfrey's lip trembled. "All those years of suffering at the hands of Shanks... then that miracle... stock-piling my retirement fund... and now... all that... for a measly hundred and twenty-five grand!"

"Oh, stop whingeing, Godfrey!" interrupted Soppy.

* * *

Godfrey hadn't managed to utter another word. He remained silent, his mind in a distant land of 'what might have been'. Arty continued addressing the crowd. He told them of Godfrey's 'tireless, devoted efforts' for West Mayling House over the years. He mentioned the new buildings... the new facilities... and all that "damned expensive technology – as the Headmaster calls it!"

The tale of Godfrey's imminent departure finally left most of the audience weeping in gratitude – and deep sadness at the school's "great loss," as Arty put it.

'Great loss?' thought Sid with a smile.

Arty could hardly contain himself. Tears of laughter streamed down his face. If only they knew the truth...

Godfrey, meanwhile, blubbed helplessly... but his were tears of misery.

Trying hard not to split his sides, Arty led the crowd with... "Three cheers for Godfrey."

"Hooray!.. Hooray!.. Hooray!" boomed the parents, who burst spontaneously into... "For he's a jolly good fellow... And so say all of us!"

Now, all one hundred and eighty students were crying uncontrollably. Parents were worried at how distraught their beloved offspring seemed to be. The truth, however, could not have been further afield. The fact was – they'd never laughed so much in their lives!

They were delighted... euphoric... victorious!

* * *

The crowd eventually began to disperse. Arty and the other six didn't hang around either. They didn't want to get caught in a discussion with parents – or the Police – on why Godfrey had resigned. They certainly didn't want the Chief Superintendent to know about the rebellion, the embezzlement of funds, or the 'arrangement' that they'd struck with the Head. Nor did they want to discuss who could possibly replace Godfrey.

Little did anyone know that a new Headmaster *was* waiting just around the corner. After the Easter Holidays, a new era would dawn upon West Mayling House...

* * *

The seven friends walked casually back to the Main Building. There, they greeted their colleagues. Hugs were dished out all round and everyone eagerly swapped stories about what had happened that eventful day.

The teachers were sitting on the grass next to the Pavilion looking a little the worse for wear. Arty peered over at them. He thought that, with the odd two or three – maybe four – forced to resign along with their Headmaster, their school would become a much better place.

That had been his whole intention.

Sure, he'd enjoyed the teachers' pay-back lessons. Deep down, however, it had been the improvement of conditions at school that had been his main concern. He smiled and turned to his friends. They were all looking at him.

"So where's the million quid, Arty?" asked Soppy. "I can't see the Police with it."

"Absolutely not! That belongs to West Mayling."

"Agreed... but..."

"Brains took care of it."

"How?"

"Just after Shanks was whacked with the painting, Brains leaped into action. First, he unplugged the CCTVs, so no-one could watch what he did.

"Yes. Then I replayed the video and saw that Shanks had his back to the camera all the time. So you can't actually see how much money he stuffed into his sack."

"So what?" asked Sid.

"So no-one knows what the real amount was in Godfrey's safe."

"So what?" asked Sid again.

"Well, I wanted to rescue that money. Like Arty said, we want it for our school. I grabbed Shanks' sack, emptied the notes out and stuffed them inside Devinia's desk."

"Oh – that's really safe!" mocked Sid.

"I didn't leave them there," tutted Brains. "When

286

the Police had gone out – I raced them up to our dorm and stuffed them under Mitch's mattress. No one's going to search there, are they? It literally is *safe!*"

"Ha, ha!"

"But I did leave a hundred thousand downstairs inside the sack," added Brains.

"Why?"

"Because the Police *would* have expected to find that amount on Shanks. That's what Tony told them when he made that fake call yesterday. Now they've caught him red-handed – money and all."

"And this means we *will* scoop any reward that's going *and* get the hundred thousand back, too!" grinned Tony.

"Which we can use to pay off Godfrey," declared Arty. "Then he can set sail into the sunset, a free man, away from West Mayling for life."

"Hang on a minute," said Soppy. "Is he *really* a free man? Won't Shanks spill the beans on him to the Police?"

"Unlikely," interrupted Tony. "My guess is that Shanks will keep his mouth shut. He'll do his time in jail and come out in a few years thinking he can continue this 'relationship' with Godfrey. After all, it's making him money."

"And he doesn't suspect Godfrey of being involved in setting him up," explained Arty. "He thinks it was just us."

"Great!" scoffed Sid. "So when he does get out of

jail and finds out he's broke, he'll come our way looking for revenge!" He looked down at his feet and sulked. "Blimey! I really don't fancy being cut up and mailed through the post!"

The students laughed. Arty gazed around the group. He realised none of their success could have been achieved without the support of each other. These were going to be friends for life.

What a team!

It was *their* victory.

They deserved it.

* * *

Godfrey Mannering looked around at his school, probably for the final time.

He thought about the rebellion, the name-calling, the capture of his staff and the way it had all been co-ordinated by the children. He thought back to the re-enactment of the battle and the other lessons he was forced into himself. He re-lived the humiliation of it all, the Art Lesson, the celebratory meal, even worse... that blessed ballet performance.

He looked at Arty and the others.

He guessed that those pesky brats would be feeling very pleased with themselves. He hated that. He scowled – they were once so restrained, tamed, kept in order and silent.

Where had it all gone wrong?

Above all, he thought about the defeat. He'd been wounded. He'd been beaten and humbled... he didn't like it one bit. He scowled one last time.

* * *

The Chief Superintendent accompanied Godfrey as they made their way back to the Main Building. The Chief glanced over at the group of children huddled together and turned to speak to the Head.

"Ah, Headmaster, I've been hearing about what some of your pupils did during the capture of Rory Shanks. Quite a *resourceful* bunch of children you have here... wouldn't you say?"

"*Resourceful?*" muttered Godfrey Mannering, "The children are *resourceful? Revolting* more like! The children are definitely revolting!"

THE END

Other Books by
Jon Turley

So was that the end of Mannering? Where did he go to retire? Did the Detective Chief Superintendent ask him any awkward questions about Shanks?

And how come West Mayling's new Headmaster was "waiting just round the corner?"

Fortunately, the adventures of Arty Fox and his friends don't stop with *The Children are Revolting*. You can follow their later exploits in...

The Doomed Prince, and
The R.A.T.T. Pack

Other titles in the Turley Tales series include
Empty Pages

Turley ● Tales

The Robinswood Press
www.robinswoodpress.com